Angels and Devils

Angels and Devils

William Wilson

Best wishes
William Wilson

Bridge House

British Library Cataloguing in Publication Data
A Record of this Publication is available from the British Library

ISBN 978-1-914199-24-0

This edition published 2022 by Bridge House Publishing
Manchester, England

For Chris, the most exciting story of all.

CONTENTS

ANGEL OF MERCY 8
CAMERA OBSCURA 11
COLLATERAL DAMAGE 15
SOMEONE LIKE YOU 42
MYXOMATOSIS 59
DOUBTS AND BENEFITS 66
SNIP, SNIP 97
THE LODGER 99
MATEUS ROSÉ 122
FOR RICHER FOR POORER 132
NATIVITY 160
ABOUT THE AUTHOR 163
LIKE TO READ MORE WORK LIKE THIS? 164
PLEASE LEAVE A REVIEW 165

ANGEL OF MERCY

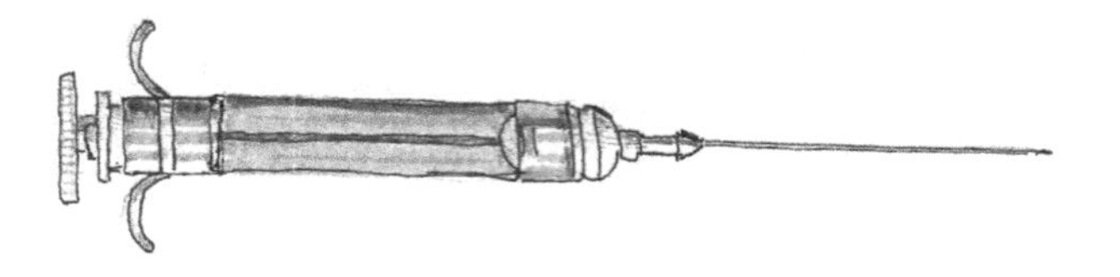

'I don't know what I'm doing here,' she says. 'It's not as if I can make any difference.'

She is standing by a bed. It has a rusting cast-iron frame, a thin mattress and a red-cross blanket. The woman in the bed, not much more than a teenager, with livid burn marks across her face and arms, is moaning and trying to remove the bandages around her eyes. Outside there is the thump of artillery and the occasional crack of rifle fire.

'You always make a difference,' I say. 'Look at me.'

She faces me, a mask over her nose and mouth, her hands gloved, her eyes cast down as if looking for a hiding place in the floor. I place my hands on her shoulders.

'Look at me.' I shake her shoulders gently. 'Come on.'

Slowly she raises her gaze, large soft eyes tilting upwards, tears rimming the lower lids, bulging outwards, waiting to fall. She angrily scrapes them away with the back of a sleeve and blinks a couple of times.

'You just have to get through this,' I say. 'Think about your place here. We cannot manage without you. Really. If you give up, then we might as well all go home.'

'But there's nothing we can do to help these people,' she says. 'They may as well already be dead.' She gestures towards a tiny baby with its huge head and staring eyes and little twigs of arms, its withered legs drawn up to its belly in a tangle of pain.

'There's not much I can do for this little fellow,' I

say, 'but you will give him love, you will help him in his final moments, and this woman here.' I look at the old lady in the bed behind us, curled up asleep, breathing evenly. 'We have saved her. Remember the story of the starfish?'

'What's the story of the starfish?' she asks. She knows I love telling stories.

'There was a man walking along a beach after a tidal surge on the Massachusetts coast,' I begin. 'There was hardly anyone about. There'd been warnings the day before to stay away from the shore, but the danger was over now. Among the flotsam and the stinking seaweed there are thousands of starfish washed up above the tideline. He sees a young boy, tousle headed, rough clothing, no shoes, picking up one of the starfish and preparing to throw it into the sea.

'Whatever are you doing?' says the man. 'There are thousands and thousands. You can't possibly save them all.'

The boy doesn't answer, just looks at him as if he is stupid, then he takes a little run forward and throws the starfish as far as he can out to sea.

'I saved that one,' he said.'

'Hmmm. And what about him?' the nurse says, removing her mask and pointing to a bed beside the wall, her pretty mouth downturned in distaste. The rebel soldier is propped up on pillows, bloodied bandages binding his chest, a deep cut across his right cheek carving an ugly 'V' across his ear, a crazy paving of stitches and sutures. 'What are we saving him for?'

'We must not take sides,' I say. 'We are all God's creatures. We must have compassion for everyone.'

'But when he leaves here, he will go on to kill and rape and maim more than we can possibly save,' she says.

‘We must not take sides. You know that.’

I can see her looking at the soldier. He is strong despite his wounds. He looks back at her, eyes narrowing. There is another rumble of artillery fire, getting closer, and he grins. She is thinking, chewing her lip. She looks brighter; suddenly a new perspective has opened.

‘You’re wrong,’ she says to me, very matter of fact; there is no argument; she is very sure of herself. ‘We cannot stand and watch. It’s a bit like the starfish. We have to act.’

Smiling now, the nurse strokes my arm as if to comfort me, to reassure me, and takes the key from her apron pocket and picks her way between the beds to the locked cabinet near the operating table. She unlocks the cabinet, takes out a ridged green bottle and loads a syringe from it, enough to kill a horse. She looks back as if daring me to make a move. She goes over to the soldier and holds his hand, caresses his forehead and makes soothing noises in his good ear. He closes his eyes. She takes his arm and pushes the needle deep into the muscle.

Published in anthology *Twisted Tales,*
Ragingaardvarkpublications 2016

CAMERA OBSCURA

'Stop,' I yelled, 'stop,' but whoever it was took no notice and I broke into a run after them. I reached the breakwater and scrambled over it. The sand was firmer on the other side and I could run faster, but I was shocked to see the thief was a girl, about the same age as me. She was skinny and had dark hair. She'd got my camera in her hand and the strap was dangling from the case. I'd left it on the breakwater while I went for a swim.

I shouted again and ran even harder but there was no way I could catch her until she stopped, turned and looked back. I slowed down. She was barefoot, and just stood there unafraid, letting the camera swing to and fro so it was nearly scraping the sand. Her mouth was curled up in a sneer. I knew she must be one of the children from the caravan site at the end of the beach. I was never allowed to go there. My Grandma thought they were gypsies, foreigners. The girl looked sideways at me, spat into the sand. I'd never seen a girl spit before. It was a calculated insult, her tongue poked between her lips to release a thick gob of mucus.

I stood half-bent over with my hands on my hips, breathing heavily, and when I looked up I saw her properly for the first time. She was taller than me, dark skinned as if she lived outside. She wore a thin skirt with a flowery pattern which hung half-way down her shins and was soaked and heavy with dirt. It clung wetly to her backside, and she had a grubby white sun top several sizes too small, a hint of breasts pushing out the fabric across her chest.

'D'yer wanna look?' she said, making a pretence of yanking the sun top up above her stomach.

'No,' I muttered, looking down, a strange jellylike feeling in my abdomen, like going over a roller coaster. My pulse raced.

'I want my camera back,' I said boldly. It was a Kodak Instamatic 127, brand new. 'Pleeease,' I said. My voice croaked like a frog.

'What's it worth?' she said.

'I don't know, it's a birthday present,' I said, misunderstanding the question. She took immediate advantage.

'How old are you?'

'Thirteen,' I said, looking down again, conscious of my podgy body and short hair. Perhaps if I answered her questions for long enough, she would tire of it and give me my camera back.

'Who from?' She was holding up the camera, making as if to drop it but then catching it by the strap.

'My mother.'

'Mother, Mother.' She imitated my voice. 'Is that what you call her then?' and, when I didn't answer, 'I bet you call her Mummy.'

'No,' I shouted, too loud and too quickly.

She smirked. 'So, what else did you get for your birthday?'

'I got some book tokens.'

'And?'

'Some money from my grandma.'

'How much,' she said, quick as a lizard.

'Five pounds.'

'Shit.'

I'd never heard anyone say that before, except for the gardener. It bored its way into my head like a worm.

I saw her relax; she knew I was not going to shout out or try and snatch the camera and run off. She was looking at me again. Lipstick smeared across her mouth like a provocation, no other make-up, black curly hair. Her face was combative, narrow eyes. No jewellery, no watch. Her bare arms were sinuous, her hands bony with bitten nails.

I felt water trickling down the inside of my leg from my swimming trunks, still wet from the sea.

'Are you pissing yourself?' she said, wrinkling her nose and smirking at the same time.

'No, I'm not,' I said loudly. 'It's from my trunks. I've been swimming.' I squirmed.

She wrinkled her nose again.

'I'm not.' I shouted.

She was staring at my crotch, and I could sense a bulge growing unbidden in my trunks. Please God she hadn't noticed. But she had. She curled her lip. I waited for the insult, but it didn't come.

Instead, she shrugged. 'Are you on holiday?' she said.

'No, we live here,' I said.

'Whereabouts?' the question snapped back.

'Humberstone.'

'I bet you live in one of them posh houses,' she said.

We didn't; we lived in an old Victorian terrace, quite smart, but not what I'd call posh so I didn't know what to say.

'Tell you what,' she said slowly, drawing a line in the wet sand with her toe and looking sideways at me. 'You want your camera back?'

I didn't answer, just waited miserably for whatever was coming next.

'Well, you can have it for a fiver.'

'I haven't got any money on me.'

‘How’re you going to get home then?’

‘My mother’s got the car down the other end by the boating lake.’

‘You can come back tomorrow.’

‘But she’ll see I haven’t got the camera.’

‘I’ll give you the case back now; you can have the camera tomorrow. Bring the money, come in the afternoon.’

‘Shall I come here?’

‘We’ll be under the pier. Me and my friend. You’ll like her. It’s near where we go swimming.’ She pretended to pull her sun top up. ‘You can take some photos if you like.’

She took the camera out and walked over to me, dangling the case on the end of its leather strap.

I took the case and turned around to run back, all the way to the carpark. I was breathless by the time I finally reached the car.

‘Darling, I was about to come and look for you. What on earth has happened: look at your shorts, your sandals, your hands.’

‘I went swimming,’ I said, ‘then I fell over by the breakwater.’

‘You’d better take those wet trunks off. Your socks and pants are in the back. There, there,’ and she wrapped me in a great big yellow fluffy towel. ‘I was starting to get worried.’

‘No, it’s OK,’ I said. ‘Really.’

She saw the camera case on the back seat. ‘Thank goodness you didn’t lose your camera.’

I pulled on my pants and shorts underneath the towel and climbed into the front seat.

‘Mummy?’

‘Yes, darling.’

‘Can we come back again tomorrow afternoon?’

COLLATERAL DAMAGE

Adrian had nearly finished. He fired twice to the head through the jeep window. Bits of brain flew out and the first of the attackers slumped over the bonnet, leaking blood over the wheel arch. Adrian pumped the air. 'Tango down. Tango down.' He now had over 40,000 points. Flinging the jeep into reverse, he drove backwards into the remaining attacker, pinning him against a wall. Not hard enough. Only fifteen seconds left. He drove forward so the guy fell into the road, then reversed over the body. 'Tango down, Tango down.' Just in time. 50,000 points. 'Yeah yeah.' New menu. Adrian saved the game and packed up the laptop, the headphones and the toggles. It was time to go, his mother had been ready for ages, but she had had to wait.

Francesca Lopez, Frances to her friends, stands in the lantern window on the upper landing looking out over the drive, waiting for them to come. It is Mid-August, a heatwave. The whole landscape is waiting for something to happen. You can see for miles from here; to the south, all the way along the river to the old fort and the sea; to the west, the village and the South Downs. Frances can see the car, an old Mercedes estate, with Nuala, her sister-in-law, at the wheel as it turns off the main road into the village. She goes downstairs and stands waiting, arms folded, head on one side, wondering how they are coping. It is five years since Jack was fatally wounded in Basra.

Adrian jumps out and opens the gates to let the Mercedes through. The old car rattles up the drive and round the pond with its ornamental fountain to the house. Adrian runs across to Frances and she kisses his forehead and ruckles his hair.

'Hola, mi amigo,' she says, 'this is a treat. Gosh, you'll soon be as tall as me.'

'Hello, Auntie.' He looks up. 'Can I go and see Snoopy?'

'I'm surprised he didn't hear you at the gate.' She shields her eyes with her hand. She is a striking looking woman, tall and slim yet strong. She has jet black wavy hair piled on top of her head, clear wide blue eyes, nostrils which flare like an animal's, and she can blow kisses like Marilyn Monroe; she's missing a tooth – an upper right pre-molar – which gives her a rakish almost saucy look when she smiles.

She puts two fingers in her mouth and gives a piercing whistle. The dog appears within seconds, bounding through the tall grass on the riverbank at the far corner of the old paddock, and finally jumping up first at Adrian and then at Nuala who's struggling to unload the car.

'Christ, it's hot.' Nuala's T-shirt is soaked with sweat. Her baggy tracksuit bottoms are creased, her mop of brown hair damp and limp.

Frances calls, 'Adrian, go and help your mother.' But Adrian has already run off with Snoopy.

'Here, let me help.' Frances tugs in vain at the tailgate. 'It really is time you got another car, Nuala, you've had this as long as I can remember.'

Nuala frowns, eyes closed, shutting out memories.

'Jack loved this car,' she says simply. 'Anyway, I can't afford another.'

'I'm sorry, Nuala, that was insensitive of me.'

'No, silly, it's me. I'm not very good company nowadays. It's really difficult on my own with Adrian. I just can't cope in the holidays.'

'Don't you worry, he'll be fine here, I'll take care of him, bless him.'

'I just hope you can get him out a bit: don't let him stay in his room all day; he's always on his computer.'

'Well, there's lots of other things for him to do here. He won't need his computer.'

'You know he's brought it with him?'

'What? Why did you let him?'

'Let him! I couldn't stop him.'

'What do you mean, couldn't stop him? He's only twelve.'

Nuala can't stay for lunch. Adrian gives her a perfunctory kiss then goes upstairs as Frances goes out with Nuala to the car.

'I'll come down with you and open the gates.'

The engine splutters a couple of times, then fires.

'Thanks again, Frances. I hope he's not too much bother. Ring me if you've had enough.'

'Don't be silly. I'll give him lots of T.L.C. You put your feet up, and don't worry. See you next weekend. Safe journey.'

Frances walks back along the drive to the house, looking up to the top floor to see Adrian's face at the window. He has no expression. She wonders quite what she has taken on.

In the early dawn on this hot humid morning, Frances lies awake on her back like a beached starfish, covered only with a sheet. She misses Julian in this huge bed. She's proud of his job with the Foreign Office but she's often anxious when he's away. Her own family were from Chile, but they had been murdered by the Pinochet regime in the 1970s. Frances still has a terror of the military. When she'd learnt Julian would have to go to Iran in August she'd hoped that having Adrian to stay would be a welcome diversion. Already she is having doubts.

She raises her knees and squeezes her legs together: she needs the loo but is reluctant to rise. Snoopy, her gorgeous daft Labrador will stir, he'll bark and want to go out, and Adrian will wake up. She prefers some time on her own first.

The previous evening had started OK. After a long walk together up the river and back, Frances went upstairs to help Adrian unpack. She put him in a cosy little room near the master bedroom where he wasn't too isolated. Most of the other habitable bedrooms were too large and grown-up for a twelve-year-old. She left him whilst she skyped Julian and prepared a meal.

'Adrian!' she called up the stairs. 'Adrian, dinner's ready.'

No response.

'Adrian.' She went up to the half-landing, now shouting.

'Adrian! Adrian!'

Nada.

She opened the bedroom door. Adrian was wired to his laptop, plugged into headphones, eyes staring, mouth bared, knuckles white on the control as if his life depended on it, which it did, given the battle taking place on the screen. Muttering constantly under his breath, 'yeah, yeah,' and had she even heard 'fuck'? She called again but he had no idea she was there until, suddenly angry, she moved forward to remove the headphones.

'No!' he shouted. 'No!' He hit out, wildly, catching her just below the navel.

'Dios mio, you have to stop; you have to stop.' She grabbed him around the chest and pinned his arms against his sides.

He slumped in front of the screen, staring at the frozen

image of a bearded Arab wearing a hijab scarf and wielding an AK47.

Frances stood over Adrian whilst he turned the equipment off and then marched him down the stairs. The dog ran up to Adrian then ran away again. Adrian was silent throughout dinner. Frances's attempts to make friends, interest him in what they might do tomorrow, gently warn against too many violent games, sank into the silence. After dinner Frances went upstairs with Adrian, removed the laptop and waited whilst he got ready for bed.

'I'm sorry you're so upset,' she said. 'Try and have a good night; let's have a nice day tomorrow. Okay?'

Frances had remained alert for any sounds from Adrian's room, but all was quiet. She spent longer than usual locking up and setting the alarms. She had slept badly, frequently waking up to imagined small stirrings and mutterings. Dawn had come as a relief.

She goes downstairs to the loo but it's no good being quiet: the dog barks madly then bolts out the door and tears off towards the paddock. She prepares breakfast, makes coffee, then showers. She examines herself in the mirror: there's a bruise where Adrian had lashed out last night. She touches her breasts and rubs a hand down her stomach, stretches up and clasps her hands above her head, bends down and clutches her ankles. She's still in good shape, fit enough to cope with a twelve-year-old. She dries herself, pins up her hair, puts on a silk blouse and tight black jeans, and walks firmly up to Adrian's door.

'Time to get up, young man.' So far so good. Adrian is awake, a bit wary, polite and almost articulate. He trots downstairs in his pyjamas.

'We've plenty of cereals, and I'll make some toast.'

'Thank you, Auntie.'

'Do you want anything else, eggs, bacon?'

'No thanks, Auntie.'

'I thought we might drive into Brighton today, go down the pier, have lunch somewhere, maybe the Iguana Bar if you promise not to ask for a tequila.'

'Yeah, sounds cool.'

Olé. Frances has scored a bullseye.

But later in the afternoon Frances's day falls apart. Adrian has some pocket money he is determined to spend. On their way to the beach after lunch they pass a "Sporting Goods" shop. Adrian is transfixed, pressed against the window. He ogles the rows of shotguns, the air pistols nestling like tinned mackerel inside their wooden boxes, the cartridge cases in regimented patterns on the plastic grass.

'Oh please, Auntie Frances, please can I just go inside?'

'Don't be silly, Adrian, there's nothing there you can buy.'

'No, I just want to look. Please, please.' He has his hand on the door.

'No, Adrian, I don't want to go in.' Guns make her feel ill; she's looking away.

But then Adrian is in the shop, looking at the racks of shotguns, going to the counter. She waits for him to be shooed out but he's pulling some money out of his trouser pocket and the shopkeeper is putting something into a bag. He runs out beaming, really thrilled.

'Look, Auntie, a catapult, a real catapult.'

'Adrian, I will not have you disobeying me like this. I told you not to go in there. Give it to me.'

'No, it's mine, mine, I bought it. It's my money. Mummy would let me have it. No, no, I won't.' He snatches his hand away from hers.

'Okay, okay,' she says, with people staring and one stupid man even asking Adrian if he's all right, 'but you can't play with it now. It's not a toy. Put it away. We'll see if there's anywhere safe you can play with it at home. Do you still want to go to the beach?'

'Yes, please, Auntie.'

'Then give it to me now, and I'll look after it. You can have it when we're back home.'

An hour later Frances is lying on a towel reading. The catapult is in her bag. Adrian sits throwing pebbles into the surf.

Back at home, Frances gives Adrian his catapult, and goes with him to the paddock. They've made some targets out of cardboard, with proper bullseyes, and threaded them with string so they can be tied to trees or fence posts. Adrian is thrilled.

'You can't just shoot at anything: you must promise me you'll be really careful, and only shoot at the targets.'

'Yes Auntie, I promise to be careful.'

'And you must never point it at a person, and never ever shoot at any living thing. Promise me, Adrian.'

'Promise, Auntie.'

Involuntarily she clutches him to her, cradles his head, strokes his hair.

'I'll call when it's time for dinner.'

She whistles for the dog and goes back to the house for her daily call to Julian. She turns on the computer in the office. Her eyes jump to the words at the bottom of the screen: 'Julian online.' The relief makes her realise how anxious she is every time she does this. She presses the call icon and his face fills the video window.

'Hola, darling.' She has always greeted him thus, ever since the beginning.

Julian asks is she is all right. 'You look worried?'

'No,' she says. 'Everything's fine. It's so hot here. How are you?'

'Missing you.'

'What are you doing?'

'Just preparing the final paperwork: big day tomorrow.'

'Do you think they'll agree?'

'I think they might.'

'Then you'll be home soon?'

'I hope so. Yes. How are you getting on with Adrian? Is he behaving himself?'

'I wish. It's fine most of the time but he gets these rages.'

She tells him about the catapult. 'At least it's keeping him occupied outdoors and away from his computer.'

'You sound to be doing wonderfully, darling. Sorry it's such a struggle: I have a feeling he's not getting any better.'

'No, it all goes back to that awful time when Jack died.' She shudders. 'It's terrible to say it, but it would have been better if he'd died instantly in Iraq, rather than those terrible wounds and all those operations back in Birmingham. And then those dreadful weeks at home before he died. God only knows what Adrian must think. I don't know how Nuala coped.'

'We'll have to talk when I get home. We must see if we can get some professional help for Nuala. Maybe Pat can recommend a really top child psychiatrist. We'll have to pay but that's OK.'

'Let's talk about it. Anyway, I'll try my best this week. I'll take him down to the fort tomorrow, then the beach: we'll go swimming. It'll be a relief in this heat. Then on Thursday we've got Oliver all day. Pat and Emma are going up to London, so they'll drop him off on the way to the station.'

'That'll be nice, won't it be a bit difficult with Adrian though? Remember that time when Oliver seemed frightened of him. We could never get to the bottom of what happened. Let's hope that Oliver has forgotten all about it.'

'Oh, he'll be all right. We'll go for a long walk or something.'

'Just so long as you don't leave them together for too long.'

'No, of course not.'

'Sorry, I know you won't. I'll be thinking of you: I won't be able to skype tomorrow – the meetings will go on all day and probably all night too. I'll call you on Thursday evening.'

After the call Frances sits awhile in the office, thinking about the single most precious person in the world, her only grandchild, baby Oliver. Perfect in every way. She aches to take him in her arms again. But she knows Julian is right with his warning. She will be careful.

The old house creaks in the heat, Snoopy pants in the open doorway, seagulls overhead, and what's that thumping noise upstairs?

'Adrian?' she calls. 'Is that you?'

She cringes. Had he followed her into the house? Had he heard the conversation? What was he doing upstairs?

She might have guessed. As she goes upstairs, she can tell from the creaks and muffled curses that he's in the middle of another video game. It's no good shouting; she opens his door and this time, wary of any sudden reactions, makes sufficient noise for him to look up.

'Wait, wait!' he yells, 'just a minute.'

Whilst she waits, she takes in what is on the screen. So much death. So much hate. And with another bloody battle won, Adrian saves the game, takes off his headphones, and looks round at her.

'Adrian, I thought you were still outside, not inside on a day like this. I don't like you doing this – all these games.'

'This is the first time today. We've been out all the time.'

'Yes, and you've had a good time, haven't you? Where's that catapult?'

'I've put it away.'

'Okay then, you can play a bit more until dinnertime, but that must be it for today.'

Then, just as she is leaving to go downstairs, she asks, 'You didn't listen to me on skype to Uncle Julian did you?'

'No.' As he looks away, he leans over to pick up the headphones.

'Are you sure?'

He frowns. 'No.'

They clear away after dinner and go round the paddock and along the riverbank with Snoopy in the fading light.

'Auntie?' he says as they're returning to the house. 'I haven't got any credit left on my phone. Can I phone Mum when we get back?'

Privately relieved, and determined to avoid any hint of getting the credit renewed, she says, 'Of course you can. Do you want to use the phone in the office?'

Afterwards she asks whether he wants to watch the TV, or a video, but no, he wants to go upstairs again.

'Adrian, I'm not having you playing any more of those video games tonight. It's not good before going to sleep.'

'I won't Auntie, I promise.'

'Then what will you do? Will you read?'

'Yes.'

'What book are you reading?'

'I don't know, it's new.'

'You not going on that computer, are you?'

'Not to play games. Not tonight. I want to look on Facebook.'

'Okay. Half an hour, but no more. I will come up at ten o'clock and you can get ready for bed.'

She is as good as her word, and Adrian gives in. She waits whilst he goes in the bathroom. She puts out his pyjamas, looks away when he gets undressed, folds his jeans and t-shirt over her arm, tucks him up and sits down on the bed beside him.

'You know we love you,' she says, stroking his hair. 'We'll always love you.'

'Night night, Auntie.'

'God bless.'

At breakfast the next morning, out of the blue, Adrian asks, 'Auntie, some friends of mine are staying in Newhaven. Can I go and see them?'

'What? Who are they? Do I know them?'

'No, Auntie, they're just friends. They're on holiday.'

'Where are they staying? Are they at an hotel?'

'They're staying at someone's house.'

'Well, whose house?'

'It's their aunt and uncle's.'

'Does your mum know about these friends?'

'I think so.'

'Well, does she or doesn't she? I'd better give her a ring.'

'No, Auntie, it doesn't matter, it was only an idea.'

'Well, let's forget about it. I thought we could take a picnic and drive down to the old fort. There's the amusement park; we can go to the beach, have a swim. How would you like that?'

'That'd be cool, Auntie.'

It is hot climbing up the earth cliffs to the old fort, but great fun too, the channel stretched out below, gulls mewling and crying in the wind; there's a big dodgems beside the beach, flashing lights, a smell of rubber, the boom-boom of heavy rock music. Adrian races around crashing into everyone else; there are shrieks and yells.

Both of them are strong swimmers and as the tide comes in, they swim for ages. They wait on the breakwater to wave to the ferry from Dieppe, then finally lie spreadeagled on towels. Frances reads for a while, then dozes, the sun slowly drying her swimsuit, a few stray rivulets trickling down her thighs. She dimly hears Adrian scrabbling about on the shingle.

And then a lot of shrieking and cawing and someone – Adrian? – running, crash, crash, crash over the stones on the other side of the breakwater. He jumps down beside her a bit breathless.

'What is it?' Frances gets to her feet, looks around, then, with mounting suspicion looks over the breakwater. She cries out in shock. A large herring gull is floundering on its side, one wing beating at the wet shingle, its beak pecking furiously at the other wing, broken and twisted underneath. Helpless, the gull is pushed up the beach by each incoming wave, to be left stranded on the wet pebbles. Frances scrambles over the breakwater and sprints across, feet slipping on seaweed and bruised by the stones. Her heart is thudding painfully, breath coming in short gasps. She kneels in the foam and tries clumsily to gather the bird up into her lap, but it is no use; there is blood amongst the torn feathers, the gull's head already flopping uselessly against Frances's knees. She stands up, looks around, and not knowing why, she walks out through the surf holding the dead bird against her breast, then slowly lowers it into the water, back into the sea.

Frances walks back to where Adrian is sat, unmoving, on his towel, rucksack at his side.

'It was you, wasn't it?' she says quietly, her voice trembling.

'No-o.' He draws out the word, voice rising.

'Give it to me: give me the catapult.' And before he can move, she reaches down into the rucksack, tears it open, sees the catapult lying there at the top, still wet, and snatches it up.

'It was an accident; I was only playing.'

He is shouting, reaching up to grab the catapult back, but she is too quick for him. He's still scrambling to his feet when she runs down again to the water's edge and hurls the catapult with all her strength into the air. It arcs high over the water, glinting in the sun, and drops far out into the sea.

She climbs back up the gravel and grabs him by the shoulders, trying to look into his eyes, but he looks away. She shakes him.

'Madre de dios: what makes you do such a wicked, wicked thing? Why, Adrian, why? How could you be so cruel?'

She pushes her fingers through her hair and wipes tears from her eyes, shaking all the while.

'I didn't mean to hurt it,' he says. 'Don't cry, Auntie,' now crying himself, but more with bitterness than remorse, eyes narrowed, head turned, staring into the distance.

'Pick up your things,' she says, her voice flat. 'Go to the car.'

She follows behind him, dumps their stuff in the car boot.

'Get in.'

And she drives home in silence.

Snoopy comes running down the long driveway to greet them. Adrian gets out to open the gates and Frances drives up to the house, Adrian trailing along behind.

'Go to your room,' she shouts, 'and no playing on that computer.'

As Adrian drags his feet upstairs, she dives into the office and switches off the modem.

Mechanically she hand-washes the swimming things, feeds Snoopy, and then goes out around the paddock with him, watching him pushing into the hedgerows, scampering hopefully after rabbits, nuzzling his wet nose against her bare legs. She rubs the top of his head. She's starting to calm down, feeling more in control of herself.

She returns to the house to prepare for dinner, pausing to phone Emma and check what time they're bringing Oliver in the morning.

'Is 8.00 o'clock too early?' Emma asks. 'You're sure you don't mind? I'll bring everything you'll need, nappies, suncream, change of clothes. How are you getting on with Adrian?'

'Oh Emma, I think he's worse than ever. I wish I could help him more. He's carrying such a lot of anger and hurt; I can't bear to see him like this.'

She daren't mention the seagull, just adds, 'I wish I could just cuddle him up and make it better, but it's really difficult to reach him.'

'You're sure you'll be able to cope with Oliver? We could go to London another day.'

'Oh no. Don't spoil your plans. We'll be OK. It's much easier with this fine weather. We'll go for a long walk, take a picnic.'

She calls Adrian when dinner is ready, calls again, and finally he comes downstairs. She wants to make things better but can't forgive the day's events and the meal passes with no exchanges other than mere politeness. When Adrian goes upstairs again Frances is relieved. She'll wait awhile, clear away the dinner things, sort herself out and get ready for Oliver coming in the morning, and then go up to Adrian and try to bring some peace into the house before the night.

But it is not to be. At ten o'clock, just as she is steeling herself to go upstairs, the telephone rings. She picks it up.

'Hello?' she says.

A pause, then, 'Can I speak to Adrian, please?' A male voice, polite, well-spoken.

'Who is this?'

'I'm a friend of Adrian.'

'How did you get this number?'

'Adrian gave it to us.'

'When? Who are you?'

There are noises in the background, a general din, raised voices.

'Where are you speaking from?' she asks.

Is that whispering she can hear, giggling, in amongst the hubbub?

'Who shall I say is calling?'

'Tell him his Dad wants to speak with him.'

At first, she thinks there must be some dreadful mistake, some awful coincidence, but then she realises, and her whole body goes cold. She cries out again, 'Who are you? Hello? Hello?'

No response. The line goes dead.

Now fully alert, she dials 1471 but doesn't recognise the caller's number. She can return the call by pressing 3. It rings and rings then finally stops. She replaces the receiver and stands looking out of the window into the gathering darkness. What can she do? It's no good phoning the police, and Julian's in Iran. The obvious person to call is Nuala; at least she might know who these strange friends of Adrian's are, and she needs to tell her about the seagull. She calls Nuala's number, but there's no response. Frances is alone. Her hand goes over her mouth. She nibbles the cuticle of her index finger. More minutes go by. She could phone Patrick and Emma – they're only ten minutes up the road – but Patrick would insist on coming over and staying the night, and he's probably only just come off shift at the hospital. She's loath to disturb him, and anyway she'll see them in the morning when they bring Oliver.

Adrian is on the edge of sleep when she knocks quietly on his door. She walks over to the bed; his eyes open unexpectedly and he stares at her. She turns away and walks slowly, deliberately and silently out of the room.

She returns downstairs and lets the dog out. It's a sure way of knowing if there is anyone in the grounds. It's ages before he returns, but it's clear there is nothing untoward. She goes all round the perimeter of the house, first outside checking the security lights, the garages, the rivergate and the boathouse, the main gates, her hands fumbling with the catches; then inside, checking every window and every door, pausing each time to look outside. No matter how many times she checks she cannot convince herself there is no-one there. She sets the alarms knowing that she will spend the night waiting for them to be activated.

During the night Frances drifts in and out of sleep. At one point she sits up alert, not just hot and sweaty, and has heard a door open and creaking floorboards on the landing. It's Adrian going to the bathroom. She cannot just turn over and go back to sleep until she's heard the loo flush, seen the light go out, heard Adrian's door close, and silence again. Half asleep she dreams she is on guard against whatever seems threatening outside but is unsure whether Adrian himself isn't already infected, like a victim in a vampire movie, like a virus that has wormed its way into the core of the house.

She wakes again around 4.00am. Snoopy is barking. As she gets out of bed, she can tell that the security light is on at the back near the boathouse. Squirming into a nightie and grabbing her mobile she goes downstairs in the darkness and puts a restraining hand on Snoopy who is facing down the passageway, and she trembles with anger.

'Shhhhush,' she whispers and strains her ears in the silence. Nothing. She waits. After a few minutes the security light goes out. No other lights come on, and Snoopy stops trembling. Frances reaches out to deactivate the alarm and open the side door. Her hands sweat. She stands on the step and looks around. One of the empty milk bottles has been knocked over. Was it a badger, or a fox, or was it something else? Her mind turns over. She will never know, but it's no longer possible to return to bed. It's another warm and humid night and Frances would only lie there alert and waiting for Snoopy to bark or the security lights to come on again. She's cool in the nightie with her bare feet on the stone kitchen floor and already the sky is lightening over the river. She'll make a cup of tea, prepare as much as possible for the day ahead, have an early breakfast, maybe take Snoopy around the paddock in the misty dawn. And later, even that pleasure is tinged with menace: the gate between the paddock and the riverbank is open. She knows she had closed it the evening before.

'Patrick, Emma.' Frances gives a massive sigh of relief and runs across the gravel to the car, flings her arms around Patrick. Adrian, as usual, hangs back in the doorway.

'Sorry if we're a bit early… Hi, Adrian!'

'No, no, it doesn't matter, it's good.'

She struggles to hide her worries but g*racias a dios, thank God*, at last the night is over, the new day can begin.

'Are you sure you're all right?' Patrick holds on to her arms, his forehead creased in a frown.

'I'm fine.' She runs a hand through her hair and turns away. Emma extracts Oliver from the car seat and hands him, arms outstretched, to her.

'Mi pequeno.' She cuddles him, a bundle of soft smooth plumpness, and carries him up the steps into the house, murmuring into his ear, kissing his forehead. Patrick and Emma follow, laden with all the paraphernalia of modern parenthood.

'Show me again about the buggy.'

Frances always has difficulty putting it up; Patrick struggles with the mechanism. 'It has to click into place, there. Oh, and you need to be careful about the brake; the lever has to go all the way down. Sometimes I think I've put it on but then find I haven't.' He looks around. Adrian is still lounging against the front door.

'How are you managing with Adrian?' he whispers.

She lowers her voice. 'I need to talk to you about him, but not now.'

They hasten to depart, trailing reminders as they go: 'His dinner's in the cool bag… just warm it up… the water's in the side pocket… spare clothes are in the brown bag… don't forget the suncream.'

This is always a favourite moment for Frances, these first few minutes of reunion before Oliver will wriggle to get down and find his toys. She sits on the sofa cradling Oliver, gently removing one by one his little shoes then his socks, stroking his hair, feeling his weight and warmth in her lap, her eyes now closed, her other senses, touch and smell, gathering him in.

'Ganma,' he says, holding up his blue teddy. 'Oli teddy.'

'Yes,' she says, 'Oli's teddy.'

But the spell is broken: she can hear Adrian behind her.

'Hello, you,' she says. 'Look who we have here, your little nephew.'

Adrian had last seen Oliver a year ago when Oliver was only a few weeks old. Frances watches to see how they react to each other now.

'Can he talk?' Adrian sticks his face in front of Oliver's.

'A little,' says Frances.

Adrian tries to take Oliver's hand, but Oliver pulls it away and his face starts to pucker. Frances sweeps him up.

‘There, there, Oli, this is your big cousin, Adrian. He wants to say hello to you.’

Carrying Oli with one arm she pulls the highchair to the table. ‘Do you want to have breakfast? We can give Oli a few rice cakes while we eat.’

‘Okay, Auntie.’

She gives a quick sidelong look at his face but can’t read anything in it.

‘What are we doing today?’

‘Well, we’ll be looking after Oliver, won’t we? Not much this morning, but after lunch I thought we’d go for a walk along the towpath: Oliver can have his sleep in the buggy. If there’s time, we could walk all the way to Newhaven and come back on the bus.’

Adrian doesn’t respond, and after breakfast he goes back upstairs. Later she will make a cursory and futile attempt to persuade him outdoors. Otherwise, her morning with Oliver is a delight.

Trouble comes at lunchtime.

‘Auntie?’ Adrian’s eyes look hopeful. ‘Can I stay here when you take Oliver for a walk?’

‘Of course you can’t. I’m not going to leave you here on your own. Anyway, a nice long walk will do us good. You can bring your swimming things if you like, you may be able to swim in the lake.’

‘Please, Auntie, I can look after the house. I don’t want to go for a walk.’ He’s starting to mumble.

‘I said “No”, Adrian. I’m not leaving you alone in the house. I couldn’t anyway, it’s not legal.’

‘No-one would know.’

‘That’s not the point, but anyway you heard what I said. No.’

‘I could look after Snoopy.’

'Don't be silly. He's coming with us.'

Typically, when he runs out of argument he doesn't respond. He puts a foot on the stairs, grabs the banister.

'Just a minute.' A thought has occurred to Frances. 'Yesterday, when you went to phone your Mum, you didn't phone anyone else, did you?'

'No-o.'

'It's just that someone phoned last night; they said you'd given them this number.'

Adrian reddened.

'Who was it, Adrian?'

'I don't know, do I?'

'And you're sure you phoned your Mum?'

'I said I did.'

'Well, I'm going to phone her later, so you'd better be telling the truth.'

Adrian has a hunted look as he hauls himself up the stairs.

'We'll be ready in fifteen minutes,' she shouts up after him.

The river is corralled between enormous earth banks on its journey to the harbour at Newhaven. Rising with the tide it creeps inland, swirling and rolling over the groynes and timber piling, and then reverses and rushes back to the sea exposing slippery black mud, dark green weeds and rotting debris in its wake. The old towpath skirts the back of Frances's and Julian's house and across the ramp of the boathouse before running along the wide top of the earth bank overlooking the river to one side, and open meadowland on the other.

It is another hot bright day. You can see for miles from the towpath. There is no-one about, just a few ramblers on the other side of the river. Frances has been walking for about half an hour pushing the buggy. Oliver is asleep under his sunshade. The river is full and barely moving, waiting for the ebb. Adrian has been dragging behind chucking stones into the river. It had been a dreadful struggle to get him to come. At first, he had refused to leave his room when Frances had called up.

'You can't make me,' he shouted.

'Don't think you can stay here and play on your computer,' Frances shouted back. She had turned off the server in the garage to the accompaniment of more shouts of protest.

'If you come now, you can play some more when we get back. Otherwise, I'll just have to phone your mother and get her to come and take you home. Come on Adrian, please. You're not an infant. Do this for me.'

Finally, he comes, but he remains resentful, keeping his distance from Oliver, grudgingly accepting a lemonade, gulping it down and chucking away the can.

'Adrian, pick it up, give it to me.' Frances is becoming used to his studied lack of interest, the puzzled looks, the frowns, scratching the back of his head. When he looks at her, it's often a knowing look tinged with suspicion. Frances can sense him behind her, a kernel of malignancy wrapped up in a young boy, like rabies in a much-loved dog. Now he has started throwing sticks into the river for Snoopy, who charges down the muddy bank and throws himself into the water sending the ducks flying, hauling himself out and scrabbling back up to the towpath to shower everyone with muddy salt water. It hardly matters in this heat, but Frances has other concerns. Snoopy's growling is becoming more laboured and less playful as the game goes on, his wrestling with Adrian to give up his sticks becoming less determined.

'Not too rough,' Frances exclaims more than once,

looking around, and 'let him keep it if he wants,' but all to no avail. A few minutes later she hears more splashing as Snoopy retrieves another stick, then more growling growing in intensity, now higher in pitch and suddenly punctuated with a series of yelps. She spins around to see Adrian holding the dripping stick and Snoopy struggling down the bank towards the meadow, limping, dragging a hind leg.

'Snoopy!' she yells, and the dog pauses, then sits down heavily in the long grass, whimpering. She puts the brake on the buggy and charges down the bank, kneeling beside the wet shivering dog. She tries to help him up, but one hip is twisted backwards; he cannot get back on his feet. She sees his back is broken.

'Adrian,' she shouts. What have you done?'

There is no answer. Adrian is nowhere to be seen. She must get help; her mobile is in the buggy. And as she scans the top of the bank, terror strikes into her soul. Where is the buggy? She flings herself back up the bank, gasping with the effort. At the top she looks frantically along the towpath towards Newhaven – it's empty – then back the way they had come – nothing again. Whimpering with awful premonition she looks toward the river, scanning the water this way and that. Her whole body goes cold; there's something rising up then slipping down under the surface: a pair of wheels. The buggy is upside down in the water, drifting slowly downstream towards an old wooden jetty.

Her scream rises into the cloudless sky and sinks into the landscape. She thinks she sees someone; a man in a white hat looks up from the field beside the towpath as she kicks off her sandals and half runs half falls, slipping diagonally down the sludge and straight into the water. The river closes over her head, water fills her nostrils, slime clings around her jeans, sediment sucks at her feet; she strikes out, breaks the surface, sees the buggy drifting just beyond her reach; more fighting than swimming she lunges sideways and grasps a wheel; now underwater, now above, she kicks and squirms and twists. Drifting past the jetty she grabs the end of a broken timber spur, and she pulls and pulls, her outstretched hand slipping on the green timber, grabbing a giant rusted iron bolt protruding from the wood, tearing skin but finding purchase. She twists around, now wedged against the jetty by the current, gasping and coughing salt water, but the buggy is still upside down. She refuses to lose hope: hanging onto a wheel with one hand she hauls herself along the jetty, timber by timber, until she feels the mud bank below her feet. She forces herself below the water again, feeling along the buggy's frame, finally finds the pushbar, hauls it first sideways then, changing her grip, and standing with water up to her waist, she wrestles it upright, a mess of fabric and metal and in the midst of it, still buckled into the straps, Oliver, lifeless. There is no-one around. Her mobile is at the bottom of the river.

Lifeless? She will not give up. She struggles with the buckle release, weeping with frustration, pulls Oliver's cold little body out of the straps, staggers out of the river and up to the grass bank with him in her arms. His arms flop uselessly, his head lolls backwards: she lays him down on the slope, head lowest, kneels. She is shivering in the heat, soaked, bleeding from hands and feet and an awful tear in her side, but she manages to tilt Oliver's little head back, a finger under his chin, mouth over his. She puffs gently. There is an acrid salty taste on her lips. Five rescue breaths she remembers. Water runs from his mouth, but otherwise no movement, nothing. Chest compressions must follow. She is all pain and fear, two fingers on the cold little breastbone twice per second, she remembers, tries to shout it out, one… two… three… four, but loses track. Blood from her hands smears over Oliver's white skin, and nothing. Her eyes are wild, pupils focussed on Oliver's little chest – still nothing. Two more rescue breaths – nothing. She screams, furiously shaking her head, bellowing like an animal, then more compressions, one… two… three, and loses count again, and still nothing, and all the while trailing strands of her childhood… madre de dios… aduyamé… her vision blurs, she loses count, becomes giddy, her stomach heaves and she leans to the side. Bile spills from her mouth. She collapses, spreadeagled over the bank, gasping for air, sinking into darkness.

Slowly she becomes aware of a terrible throbbing, beating noise, growing ever louder, massive turbulence as all the air is sucked away then blasted back, tearing at her hair and flattening the grass. There's a helicopter on the towpath, like a giant orange insect, spilling out men in helmets and boots and high-visibility jackets, manhandling stretchers and equipment as they come, someone bending over Oliver's tiny body, wrestling with an oxygen cylinder. She tries to raise herself but there's a man in blue overalls leaning over her, wrapping her in shiny foil, lying her down again on her side, unrolling lengths of gauze, binding huge swabs around her middle, bandaging her feet.

As soon as he lets go, she tries to rise again, trying to reach Oliver: hearing these whimpering and coughing sounds, are they coming from him, can he still be alive?

Someone shouts above the noise, 'Leave him to us, darling, he's going to be all right.'

She throws herself forward, but they will not let her near.

And meanwhile there is a new commotion, more shouting,

and she sees an elderly man out of breath, pointing, his hand trembling, the man with the white hat she'd seen before she went into the river.

'Was it you called 999?' a paramedic shouts above the noise. 'You said you saw a boy push the buggy into the river?'

'Yes, yes,' the man yells. 'He ran away.' He shields his eyes and searches beyond the towpath.

Frances pushes the medic aside, her head swimming.

'There he is!' The man points. 'Over there.'

Frances follows the pointing finger; in the far distance she can see a boy struggling across the fields towards Newhaven.

'Oh my God. Adrian.' Everything starts to close in again. The paramedic shouts for a stretcher.

Frances wakes up in a hospital bed. Her wounds have been dressed, she's wearing a hospital gown, and a drip has been attached to her arm. Patrick is there. He leans forward and takes her hand, his face ridged with concern. As she opens her eyes she moans. Tears well up and roll down her cheeks.

'Oli?' she whispers, then louder, her eyes wide with fright, 'Oli?'

'He's all right.' Patrick squeezes her hand. 'He's alive. No permanent damage. Emma's with him now in the children's ward. We'll be able to take him home later.'

'Can you ever forgive me?' She takes in a huge breath with a gulp then starts to sob, wave after wave of agony. Patrick grabs the alarm button to summon the nurse. 'For God's sake, Frances, don't blame yourself. You saved his life, YOU SAVED HIS LIFE, and damn near lost your own in the attempt.' His lips quaver and he can't say any more.

'I thought he was dead.' She squeezes her eyes tight shut and shakes her head violently as if to expel the memories. 'Did Adrian really push the buggy into the river? Did someone say that, or am I dreaming?'

'Yes, apparently that's what the coastguard reported. Some old man saw what happened.'

'I thought I couldn't have put the brake on properly.'

'No, it looks like Adrian released it before pushing it over the edge. You know he was watching us when I was explaining to you about the brake? Do you think he had it in mind all along? He was just waiting for the right opportunity?'

'Patrick, no, that's too awful.'

'No doubt he'll have a lot of questions to answer when they find him.'

'What?'

'No-one knows where he is. The police are looking for him. Nuala's helping them. I gave them her number. She'll be staying in your house tonight. I hope you don't mind, I've given her a key.'

'Madre Dios, poor Nuala, how terrible for her.'

'I know. We must be really careful what we say. Emma doesn't want to see her, otherwise she could have stayed with us.'

Frances absorbs this information without comment. 'Does Julian know?'

'No. I don't know how to reach him.'

'He's going to skype me this evening. He'll probably phone you when there's no reply.'

'And Snoopy, do you know…?' She runs out of words.

'I'm so sorry Frances…'

She closes her eyes. Perhaps none of this is really happening, but then Patrick is getting to his feet and someone else is taking his place. Emma is there with Oli in her arms.

'Ganma, Ganma,' he says.

Emma lowers him into Frances's arms.

‘You darling boy,’ she murmurs, and stretches forward to plant a kiss on his forehead.

Adrian is tracked down the next day. The police trace the number of Frances’s worrying phone call, and it matches an address which Nuala has found of Adrian’s friends, a large private house on the edge of Newhaven. When the police raid the house it’s in a mess. They find the elder brother of one of Adrian’s school friends seemingly in charge, the younger boys drinking cider and living off bread and tinned food. The parents are away. Adrian is upstairs and is taken by surprise, crouched over an Xbox, fingers gripping the toggle, his ears covered by headphones, calling out, ‘Tango down, tango down, tango down.’

SOMEONE LIKE YOU

When I saw him, he was standing smack in the middle of the grand foyer of The Plaza, shoulders hunched like a bear as he tapped on his Blackberry. Other hotel guests, celebrities, politicians, high class call girls, bellboys and porters jostled round him like flotsam swirling round a rock. It was five years since I'd last seen him. He looked up from his phone, raised a hand to stop my advance.

'Just a minute,' he said, and finished his email, then threw a heavy arm around my shoulders.

'Phil, thanks for coming, old mate.'

His accent had changed, now a strange mix of Scottish and South African, but you still had to wait for him to finish whatever he was doing before you got his attention and with it the same affectionate familiarity. He looked tanned and prosperous but different somehow, older, a lot older.

'Thanks for inviting me,' I responded.

His big frame was bunched up in a coat.

'I thought we were eating here,' I said. 'Are we going out?'

'They're keeping me a table here, but I thought we could have a walk before dinner. Is that OK? I need some air.'

We headed across the road and down the steps to the

beach. It was cold and starting to rain. Hunched up against the wind and with the sea crashing over the shingle it was difficult to hear each other speak. He was staying at The Plaza overnight, thought he'd 'look up an old mate.' I let his bonhomie wash over me. Living on my own and short of company I'd jumped at the chance to re-live the good times, even if only for an evening. Campbell and I had worked together for nearly twenty years back in the '70s and '80s. I'd had to save his skin on many an occasion.

We had reached the steps by the pier.

'Come on,' he said, 'let's get out of the rain. I could do with a drink.'

And he hustled us along the boardwalk and into a great barn of a place, strobing lights, a smell of beer, sweat, cheap perfume.

'Hey, this is something, isn't it?' he shouted above the noise.

A fat blond woman in gold heels and a shiny red evening dress was crooning lustily into the microphone. Sweat stained her armpits.

Campbell banged me on the back. 'What's your poison nowadays? Don't tell me it's still Campari soda.'

'I'll have a small lager, thanks.'

The carpets stank. Campbell ordered a pint and a whisky chaser for himself. He'd commandeered a small table beside the stage steps. He took off his coat to reveal a fine Italian suit, crisp white shirt open at the neck, gold cufflinks. His shaved head glistened beneath the disco lights. He gulped back his beer. His bulk swamped the chair as he leaned backwards to take in the stage. The fat woman had removed her dress to loud jeers, revealing lacy underwear and fishnet tights. As she left the stage Campbell grabbed one cheek of her backside. She gave a little gasp, looked down at him, liked what she saw.

'Wanna buy me a drink sweetheart?' She leant over our

table, but with one eye on a paunchy slit-eyed man with a red neck and lumberjack shirt who was advancing towards Campbell.

'Sorry darling: not tonight.' Campbell stood up slowly, gathered his coat and raised a warning hand towards the advancing threat.

'We're leaving, sonny. Don't start something you can't finish.' He bent down to pick up his whisky, and took his time drinking it, all the while staring down the man with the red neck. Campbell could be intimidating when he wanted to be. The fine clothes didn't hide the great barrel chest straining under the white shirt. He had no neck, just folds of muscle under the bald head which looked as if it had been hammered down into his shoulders. His eyes were merciless. The red necked man had stopped and stood leaning forward, trying to look aggressive, but his face was pallid and he looked anywhere except at my companion. When Campbell pushed me towards the door and bludgeoned his way past him, he stepped aside.

Heading back to the hotel in the rain Campbell had his arm round my shoulder shouting into my ear. 'You've got it all here, haven't you?'

'What do you mean?'

'What about the women in that bar?'

'Not the sort of place I go; surely you've got that in South Africa.'

'Not white women like that, Phil, only black.'

He was clearly excited. I didn't know how to respond.

Back at The Plaza the doorman saluted Campbell in his cashmere coat and ignored me in my mackintosh as we revolved through the doors. Leaving our coats at the desk, Campbell headed for the bar.

‘I need a proper drink,’ he said, ‘before we eat. What’ll you have? Come on, not another bloody lager. I’m having a Pernod.’

I hesitated. ‘Campbell, it’s very kind. I don’t drink much…’ but before I had got the words out he had said, ‘Barman, make that two.’

The Pernod arrived, cloudy with iced water. In spite of my reservations, I revelled in the sweet cold shock of it.

‘Here’s to you, Campbell. Thanks for inviting me. You look to be doing very well for yourself.’

He shrugged. ‘I’m not as well as I look, but how are you, Phil? I was sorry to hear about Elaine. How long ago…?’

‘Four years next month.’

‘You didn’t have children, did you?’

‘No.’

‘And you’re living near here?’

‘Yeah, I’ve a flat further down the seafront.’

I didn’t want to talk about me.

‘How’s Katie and the boys?’ I said.

‘They’re all good, thanks.’

The boys were away at university, one at Harvard, one at Oxford. He went on to tell me about the house near Cape Town, three storeys overlooking the ocean.

‘There’s a private pathway to the beach,’ he said. ‘It’s quite isolated. We have a twenty-four-hour armed guard, mainly for Katie’s sake,’ he added. ‘I’m away a lot.’

‘I don’t know how you keep it up.’

He shrugged again. ‘I suppose you think I should just retire to a little flat by the seaside, do you?’

I should have been hurt, but this was typical of his manner. The pain must have shown in my face, for immediately he stretched out a hand, took my arm, looked directly into my eyes, and apologised.

'Sorry, mate, take no notice, I'm not really myself. I care about you, you know. I remember the good times. Come on, let's have another Pernod and then go and eat.'

I let it pass. There was something bothering him, gnawing away, I could tell, but I wasn't going to poke at it with a stick.

The maître d' had saved Campbell a table by the window. I wondered how he could command this level of service, how he had become so formidable. He was a bull dressed in haute-couture. Everything about him was immaculately laundered, pressed, shaped, polished. When we sat down to the meal he put on his happy face, leaning back and throwing an arm over the chair back, a hand pulling on his chin, or his head right down and his dark shiny eyes looking up, eyebrows raised, the skin rippling upwards on his forehead as he looked at the menu. He raised a finger to summon the waiter. He was irrepressible, ordering oysters and a bottle of stout followed by steak and a bottle of claret.

'You can't just have grilled fish,' he said as I ordered. 'At least have some oysters to start.'

'No, Campbell. You have them and enjoy them. I'm quite happy to sit here and keep you company.'

'What wine will you have?' he asked me as the sommelier hovered.

'Just a glass of white, thanks.'

'What? You're a different man to the one I knew. Look, they do a lovely Chablis. Have a carafe.'

'OK, the Chablis, but just a glass,' I insisted. 'Oh, and a glass of water.'

'Tap water, Sir?'

'Yes, please.'

'With ice and lemon, Sir?' There was the merest trace of a smirk.

'No, thanks.'

The sommelier turned to go, but Campbell had crooked his finger to lasso him back to the table.

'Are you trying to be funny, Laddie?'

The sommelier's face had gone white: 'No, Sir. Sorry, Sir.' He scraped his way backwards and escaped toward the kitchen.

'D'you remember that slimy waiter in Venice? Insisting that spaghetti vongele didn't need garlic?' Cambell's voice was becoming a bit slurred.

'Oh yeah, and Fergus insisted it did,' I said.

'And Peter got into a fight with the chef…'

'Was that the same trip we'd eaten all those olives and the chewed stones were in that bowl and then Linda, you know Linda from PR, tried to eat them thinking they were pistachios?'

And so on. The conversation was moving onto familiar ground, a long succession of foreign conferences and meetings, airports and hotels, restaurants and bars. Campbell became more maudlin as he became more mellow.

'I dunno what we'd have done without you, you know.' He was deep in memory, shaking his head. 'You kept us legal. We would have been in a terrible mess. D'you know what we used to call you?'

'You've told me before, the golden shovel.'

'Yeah, I've never seen so much shit cleared up so elegantly.'

'You're too kind,' I said.

'No, I mean it. I always felt as if I could sleep at night so long as you were looking after things. I could always rely on you.'

He could too. I'd given him his first job, promoted him, watched his star rise in the firmament, basked in his light and watched his back. He now inhabited a world beyond my reach. I was brought back to the present by the waiter.

'Let me do that for you, Sir,' flicking open a napkin.
'Is the steak to Sir's liking?'
'Would you like a little more bearnaise sauce, Sir?'
'More wine Sir?'
I felt we were under acute observation all the time.
'But everything's under control now, isn't it?' I asked.
'Christ, yes.'
'And business is good?'
'You could say that.' He grinned.
The dessert had arrived, and with it the first hint of why Campbell was so much the centre of attention.
'And you've now set up the Cape Development group, is that right? I saw an interview with you on Bloomberg, and there was that feature in Time magazine.'
'Yeah, things are going really well. Between you and me I was lucky with the timing.'
'So, Campbell.' I paused to get his attention, and he looked up from his crepes suzette. 'Are you going to tell me what brings you to Brighton?'
He grinned. 'I thought you'd never ask.' He waved his fork vaguely around the room. 'This.'
'What do you mean, this? The restaurant? No, surely not.'
'Philip, Philip,' he sighed. 'Not the restaurant, the hotel.'
'What do you mean, the hotel. It's long past its best.'
He smiled. 'I've just bought it.'
'You've bought it?' I echoed.
'Well, Cape Development Group.' He grinned again. 'It's a bit of a dump, isn't it, this place, begging for re-development. I closed the deal on Monday. Most of the staff know. There'll be an official announcement tomorrow.'

We ordered coffee. He'd gone quiet, looked up at me a few times. Something was coming, I could tell.

'When did you retire, Phil?'

'I took voluntary redundancy, if that's what you mean. About twelve years ago. We had enough to live on and I wanted to look after Elaine.'

'And you haven't worked since?'

'What could I do? The old firm had gone. I didn't want all the hassle of running another organisation.'

He thought for a minute and then said, 'I could use someone like you now.' It was as if the words had been dropped into a pond. Surely he wasn't offering me a job? My heart jumped and fluttered. I could have done with a bit of additional income but not a full time job again. I felt my way forward, like a blind man reaching for a chair.

'Do you mean, back in South Africa?'

'No.'

'And when you say, "someone like me", what do you mean?'

'Someone I can trust.'

I felt there was a lot that wasn't being said and I waited for him to go on, but then, suddenly cutting off the flow, he said, 'Shall we have a brandy, or perhaps a port?' He picked up the wine list.

'Not for me, thanks. I've had quite a lot already. I need to be careful.'

'Careful? What for? You've no-one else to worry about?'

He'd done it again. As soon as the words were out, he was apologising. He reached forward out of his seat and put a hand on my shoulder and I shrugged it off. He wafted the waiter away.

'I've had enough of this place. Let's go out and find somewhere livelier. We can talk later.' Before I could protest, he had pushed back his chair, got to his feet somewhat unsteadily, chucked his napkin on the table, and waded through a small gaggle of anxious waiters towards the concierge to collect our coats. He tripped as we went out through the door.

'Are you sure about this, Campbell?' I asked. 'Most of the places around here are a bit noisy, a bit sleazy.'

'That's fine by me. Where'll we go?'

'I've no idea. I don't do this sort of thing any longer.'

'Come on man, it's still early. We'll find somewhere to have a drink, then you can come back to the hotel if you like. There'll be a room going spare. We need to have a serious talk.'

So, against my better judgement, we went back out into the night and headed towards West Street. Thank goodness it had stopped raining, but it was still cold and the pavements were black and slippery, water everywhere. Large groups of youths swaggered down the street, many already drunk, the girls with hardly anything on despite the cold. There were queues around cash machines, and longer queues waiting for admission to bars and clubs. It was obvious nowhere here was going to let us past the door – we were over twice the maximum age everywhere we looked. We got trapped in a passageway by a police patrol called to break up a fight. A pair of club bouncers were attacking a youth spread-eagled on the ground, a jeering crowd looking on. Finally, the police let us through and we found a place near the Pavilion. It was a pub rather than a club, all deep red and yellow ochre, a copper panelled ceiling, ornate mirrors and chandeliers, giant fans. The place seemed full of foreign students and Campbell lurched through them, swaying towards the bar. You couldn't hear yourself speak. There was nowhere to sit. Campbell had bought beers and whiskies for the two of us, balancing them on the top of a slot machine. I was annoyed, but puzzled also.

I sipped at my beer and pushed my whisky away. 'You have it.' I said, and he just chucked it down his throat.

He had always been a hard drinker but never an unwise one. I'd never known him lose control so completely. I started to wonder if something was going badly wrong in his life. He seemed intent on destroying himself.

There was a group of students near us, kids really, pushing and giggling, beers in their hands, intent it seemed on pouring the dregs from a glass over the head of one of their number. The group swayed this way and that. Someone tripped, pulling down two or three others after him. A girl fell backwards into Campbell, who caught her round her bare midriff and then wouldn't let her go. She squirmed, bit his arm, him jerking back and knocking our drinks over, shards of glass exploding all over the floor, pools of beer. There were two burly men advancing towards the group and a general scramble to escape. I pulled Campbell towards the door and we crashed through it in a jumble of arms and legs, Campbell sprawling heavily across the kerb, half in the gutter. It had started raining again. Water poured out of a broken drainpipe across the pavement where Campbell lay. I tried to pull him upright, but he couldn't get up straightaway. When he did, he bent over, one arm still hanging onto me, and was violently sick. I felt that was probably a good thing. I tried to lead him away from the mess on the pavement and towards the seafront in the hope of finding a taxi. There was no hope of getting him back to The Plaza on foot, even if it were only a few hundred yards away.

'Good man, Philip.' He slurred. 'Good man, remember that time you saved me in Berlin, I still owe you mate.' Then, a little later, 'And what about that bar, the Blue Moon, in New York. What a shithole,' and so on. The awful thing was that I did remember, and in amongst all the squalid details, I couldn't help being excited. Meanwhile, Campbell was in a dreadful state, his cashmere coat sodden right through, vomit over his shoes and ankles, a knee showing through a rip in his trousers. But on the seafront, there was a taxi just dropping a party off. I helped Campbell into the back before the driver could object and with some embarrassment asked for The Plaza.

Even as the cabbie was pointing out The Plaza was but a short walk, Campbell regained his senses enough to intervene.

'No, Philip, no. Not The Plaza. Not like this.'

'Come on, Campbell, we've got to get you out of these clothes and cleaned up and warm.'

'Phil.' He paused. 'Mate.' He paused again. I knew what was coming. 'Can we go to yours? Do you mind, save me again, just this once. We need to talk, I've got to talk to you. It's important.'

I had no idea what he was saying, he was too far gone. But I had to admit that if he really was the new owner of The Plaza he couldn't be seen there in that state.

'All right.' Wearily I turned to the cabbie. 'Porchester Court. Far end of Hove Lawns.'

I'd sold the house and moved into Porchester Court after Elaine died. I loved the flat, its elegant rooms overlooking the sea on one side and the lawns on the other. I loved the entrance with the smart letter boxes and bell pushes, the brass handles and marbled hallways, the wood panelled lifts.

I lived on the third floor. It had been a struggle getting Campbell safely to my door. He threw up again, fortunately when we were still outside. I had to go down later with a mop and bucket and hoped no-one was looking. He was dripping wet, leaving a trail of water along the hallway and muddy puddles in the lift. He murmured all the time, variations on, 'You're a good man, Phil, dunno what I'd have done without you.' I dragged him into the bathroom and sat him on the toilet seat, then helped him off with his shoes and most of his clothes.

I knew that I should try and keep him awake and sitting

up and warm, so I wrapped him in a towelling robe I used for the beach, the only garment I had which he could get into. I helped him into the lounge and guided him to an armchair near the fire. I went to the kitchen to get the washing-up bowl – I couldn't risk him being sick on my carpet – and gave him a big glass of water which he put down with a grimace.

'You're not getting anything else. And don't keep thanking me,' I said before he had a chance to thank me again.

It got quite late and his condition seemed to stabilise. I'd put on the television news to help keep him occupied, but he asked me to switch it off.

'There's something I must tell you,' he said.

'Not now, Campbell. Look, I think we can get you to bed now. We can talk in the morning.'

'No, I must tell you now,' he said. 'I've been wanting to all evening.' He sighed. 'We can talk more in the morning but I must tell you now.' His voice was heavy, but with something more than drink.

'Go on,' I said.

'I didn't really come to Brighton to go to The Plaza. I came to see you.'

'Me?' I couldn't understand what he was leading up to. 'You came all this way to see me?' I repeated.

He peered at me through half closed eyes, looking for help. 'I'm dying, Phil.'

I was completely shocked, frozen to the chair. I must have been gaping at him. I waited.

He was in a fog and struggling to be clear of it. 'I've seen all the best doctors, had all the tests. I got the final results in London this week. I've got a tumour on my brain. They can't operate.'

I let the silence settle, leaned forward and put a hand on his arm. 'Does Katie know?'

He took a big intake of breath, looked at me and shook his head. 'No-one knows, Phil. No-one. Only you.'

He looked immensely weary. 'I need your help.'

I could see his eyelids beginning to close. I helped him to his feet and led him to the spare bedroom. 'We'll talk in the morning.'

I slept fitfully. I'd misread the signs the previous evening, the dropped hints, the reckless behaviour. Campbell probably slept like a child. He was still sleeping long after I was up and breakfasted. I wondered if he might have had any appointments. He'd said there would be an announcement about the ownership of The Plaza tomorrow and I rang them so they knew where he was.

He came into the kitchen, still wearing my towelling robe and looking grey and haggard.

'Thanks for saving me last night.' His voice was weak.

'Do you want a coffee?' I asked.

'Coffee? Yeah.'

'Anything to eat.' I had a sudden inspiration. 'I could do you some porridge.'

'Porridge?' He laughed, shook his head as if in disbelief, looked up at me. 'The real thing? Then yes.'

He sat by the window looking out to sea whilst I prepared the oats. I wondered how much he remembered about the previous evening.

'You said some pretty serious things last night,' I said.

'I told you about the tumour, didn't I?'

'Yes.' I paused. 'You said you're dying.'

'I am, Phil. They can't operate.'

'Yes, you said last night.'

'I get these terrible headaches. They say they're just the start. And I get so tired, you can't bloody believe it. Some days it's OK, like yesterday, but other days I get so weary.

All I want to do is sleep. It'll get worse and worse, and more frequent.'

'And do you know how long…?' I forced myself to look at him.

'A few months.' He started to become more matter-of-fact. 'I need help, Phil. Will you help me?'

'If I can, yes, of course, but I don't see how. Don't you need to be back home, back with your family? You need them surely, not someone like me?'

'You're right, I do, but I need to sort a few things out before I see them.' He explained he'd had a new will drawn up by lawyers in London. There was a draft copy in the room-safe in the hotel. Would I be one of the executors?

'I can trust you, Phil. You're one of the only people I know I can trust. You'd be well compensated, by the way. It's all provided for.'

I said I would. I was flattered. It was something I could do, and I genuinely wanted to help.

'I want to read it first,' I said.

'Of course. Good old Phil. Cautious to the end.' But there was more to come, I could tell. He inched towards it.

'Phil, can I ask you? I don't recall your being especially religious?'

'Not at all.' But where was this leading?

'You know about "living wills"?'

'I think so, something about not being resuscitated?'

'Sort of. It's to specify how you want to be treated if you're no longer of sound mind to make any decisions. It's called an "Advance Statement". I've had one prepared. It needs witnessing.'

'Campbell, I can't be involved in determining what treatment you receive. It's nothing to do with me. It's for you or your family to decide.'

'No, no, you don't understand. You wouldn't be involved

in any decisions at all. I just need someone to witness my signature, that's all. Someone I can trust.' There was that word again.

'OK. And this document's also at the hotel?'

'Yep.'

And still there was something else. He stood up and turned to gaze at the sea, leaning forwards, hands on the windowsill. I could see him holding his breath, then, still looking straight ahead, his shoulders sagging. 'There's a Doctor in Hove, very distinguished. He advises on assisted dying, medically assisted suicide. You've heard of Dignitas?' He turned to face me.

'In Switzerland. Yes, of course, who hasn't?'

'This Doctor is Chair of a Society which campaigns to get medically assisted suicide legalised. He runs discussion groups and provides private advice. It's something I want to explore, but I don't want to see him on my own; I want a witness, someone who'll ask the difficult questions, someone not involved, someone I can trust.'

'You want me to come with you to the meeting?'

He nodded, but I knew that wasn't the end of it.

'And after the meeting: what then?'

'That's the hard part. Phil,' and once again he looked straight at me with those dark shiny eyes. 'If I'm persuaded, and I should tell you that I'm minded to be persuaded, then I'll want someone to come to Switzerland with me.'

'Bloody hell, Campbell. You're not kidding, are you?'

He'd moved across to where I was standing and before I could react, he'd put an arm round my shoulder and then came a great bearhug, the rough towelling of the beachrobe rubbing against my cheek.

'I'm not sure it's legal,' I said through a mouthful of towelling, but even as I said it, I realised I hadn't said no: the legality was a complication, not a refusal.'

'I've thought it all through.' He released his bearhug but kept his arm round my shoulder. 'We wouldn't leave from here; I'll be coming from Cape Town. We could meet in Paris.'

'Hang on a minute. Isn't Dignitas in Switzerland?'

'It is. I thought we could have a day in Paris, stay overnight, probably at the Ritz – it's another of my hotels. We'll have a ball. No expense spared. We can go to Maxims, if you like, or what about Le Dome, then afterwards there's that great little bar in Montparnasse, Le Chat Noir, do you remember? Then next day go to Zurich by train – on the TGV, first class – it's a beautiful journey. One last trip, eh, Phil. One last trip. Whadda you say?'

I couldn't believe this was happening. I could feel myself getting excited, becoming swept up in some great event. I had been there at the beginning for Campbell, I had played a key part in building his glittering career, and now I would be instrumental in bringing it all to an end.

'When's the meeting with Dr Death in Hove? I bet you've already set it up.'

'I have, yes. Tomorrow morning. 10am.'

'Then we'd better get you some new clothes,' I said. 'We can't have you looking scruffy.'

---

775 Chapman's Peak Drive,
Western Cape,
South Africa.

May 6th.2013

Dear Philip,

I'm enclosing a clipping from The Cape Times of the memorial service for Campbell. It was a very moving ceremony, and I wish you could have been here to be a part of it.

I want to thank you for the part you played in helping Campbell during the past months. It was wonderful that he found someone like you to help him, someone he could trust. He spoke very highly of you, and I understand how difficult it must have been for you to handle such sensitive issues. I knew how close you had been when you were colleagues, but never expected you would play so large part in our lives as now.

You may be reassured to know that Campbell and I said goodbye on the beach. Afterwards I stood looking at the ocean whilst he went back to the house and the taxi waiting to take him to the airport. It was our joint decision that I did not accompany him to Switzerland. You made that decision possible for us.

I'm also enclosing a copy of the burial service, and a photograph of the grave which is on a hillside overlooking the ocean near our home. You will know of course that Campbell's body was flown here from Switzerland. The burial took place after the memorial service and was attended only by the close family.

Lachlan is flying back to England next week to resume his studies at Oxford, and I plan to come out later in June to see him and also to see the lawyers in London. I'll be staying at Browns Hotel. I'll let you know my more detailed arrangements nearer the time but hope very much to see you again during the trip. Perhaps I can come to Brighton, or is it Hove? Can you recommend an hotel?

With fondest regards,
Katie.

Published in anthology *Light in the Dark*, Bridge House Publishing 2014

MYXOMATOSIS

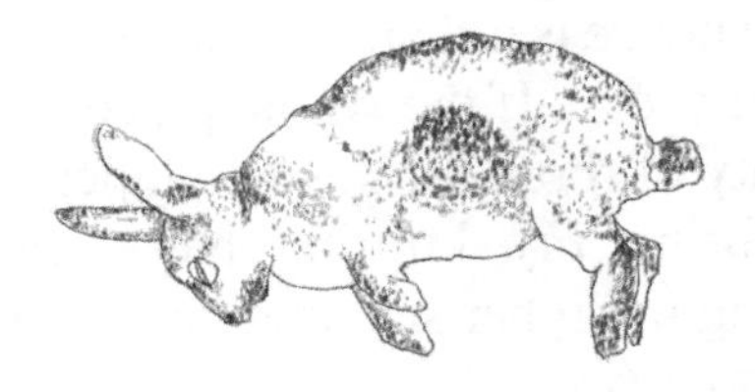

'You've just got to get on with it,' he says to himself as he approaches the junction. He turns right towards the downs and the road to Eastbourne. As the car gathers speed he leans across and places his hand gently on his mother's knee. There is no discernible reaction. She is wrapped up in herself and he is unable to undo all the layers between them. Her breath is shallow and unnaturally rapid. He withdraws his hand and presses his foot down on the accelerator. The sooner they get to Eastbourne, the sooner this will all be over.

He'd dressed carefully this morning. A suit would have been too formal but he needed a carapace of authority. The Pringle sweater and billowing Crombie overcoat should strike the right balance. He doesn't want any nonsense from the clinical staff once they get there.

'You remembered to turn off the television?' she says.

'Yes, mother,' he says. It is mid-morning, the television hasn't been on, but it is easiest to go along with it, to reassure her. In her eyes he knows he will never be competent. There will always be something left undone or done incorrectly.

'You'll water the flowers?'

It's just as well that's all she is bothering about.

'Don't worry,' he says, 'the house will be well looked after.'

'I don't like leaving it empty in the winter. You will pop in and make sure everything's all right?'

'Yes. I said don't worry about it.'

He wonders what the estate agent will say about it tomorrow. The house is a shambles but the large back garden offers plenty of scope. If the whole place is bulldozed there should be plenty of room for the developers.

'Did we bring my knitting bag?' his mother says suddenly, sitting up in her seat and clutching at his arm. He pushes her hand away.

'Careful, I'm driving.'

'Where did you put it?'

'It's on the back seat somewhere.'

His mother struggles to see and undoes the seat-belt so she can twist around. The seat-belt alarm starts to emit a high-pitched bleep.

'What's that noise?' She jumps nervously and puts her fingers in her ears.

She is simply unable to cope any longer.

'You've set the alarm off. Put your seat-belt back on.' He manages to keep his voice calm.

'Oh, Godfrey, can you stop the car? I can't go without my knitting. We must look on the back seat, or maybe it's in the boot. Please, Godfrey.' She is on the edge of tears.

He ponders what to do. If he stops and finds the knitting she'll calm down and they can proceed to Eastbourne, but if not, she'll want to go back for it. They're expecting them at the clinic at around midday. He hates being late for anything, hates being put at a disadvantage, but he can't risk his mother getting into a state. It would be so like her to change her mind at the last minute. She has lost any remaining sense of reality. Thank heavens they'd agreed these arrangements when she was still of sound mind.

'OK, we'll stop,' he says. 'Wait 'til I find somewhere to pull in.'

He finds the perfect spot, a service loop formed from a

section of the original road before the new road was built. It's near the top of the downs, wide open green pastureland dotted with sheep, white cliff faces, their edges crisp against the blue dome of the sky in the cold sunshine, gulls crying. His mother sees and hears none of it; she is fixated with the loss of her knitting. He sits for a moment, letting the engine die and the quiet take over. The car rocks gently with the gusts of wind from the channel. The parking area is empty.

A rabbit, late for the time of year, has slunk through the fence and is nibbling at the grass above the verge. Cheeky little thing. Years ago, they'd been almost completely wiped out by myxomatosis. He remembers killing an infected rabbit once. Out with a couple of friends on their bikes after school they'd encountered a rabbit with a grossly distorted face, blinded by the puffy viscous swellings around its eyes, running in circles in the lane. 'We should kill it,' he'd said, self-important, 'to put it out of its misery.' They'd found a plank of wood and he'd picked up one end with both hands and brought it down heavily on the rabbit as it scuttled around their feet. The blow had fallen on its flank and it had squeaked and whimpered but continued its frantic circling, now dragging a leg with a curious humping motion. He'd hit it again, full on the body this time, but still it didn't die, a horrid dribble of guts and blood trailing from its abdomen like a nest of worms. It lay on its side twitching, and he'd gone to look at it more closely. It was still pulsating and its mouth was opening and closing like a fish. He couldn't bear it and lifted the plank and hit it with all the force he could muster, again, and again. He never told his mother about the incident. To this day he still feels his shoulders hunch up with shame. 'We are all God's creatures,' she would have said, or something like that. Thank goodness she has lost her faith.

‘It’s here,’ he calls from the back of the car, ‘your knitting, beside your case. Do you want it in the front?’ He brings it round and puts it in her lap.

‘No,’ she says, trying to push it away. ‘I’m not going to knit in the car, you silly boy.’

‘Put it down by your feet then,’ he says. ‘I’m not getting out again.’

He knows that if he leaves it on the back seat then five minutes later, she’s going to ask again.

They top the hill at 85mph before starting the long winding descent towards Eastbourne. The nearer he gets the sooner he wants to have done with the whole business. He indicates and accelerates past a queue of cars dawdling behind a bus. Safely past he glances quickly to check his mother isn’t about to start complaining about the speed. ‘Do you always have to drive so fast?’

She says it on every journey; she has no understanding of his world. But she isn’t watching the road, she’s staring into space and there are tears running down her cheeks. He slows down.

‘Are you all right?’ he asks gently.

‘I’m cold.’

She can’t be. The car heater is on full. He’s in his shirtsleeves.

‘Inside,’ she says, ‘Godfrey. I’m cold inside.’

‘You’ll be all right once we get there.’

He is repeating words echoed from childhood, when it was he who was cold and his mother who comforted him. It was his first term at boarding school. He was eight. His father was away. He was always away. They had driven for two hours to get there in his mother’s Wolseley, a lovely car with its walnut panels and leather seats. As they approached Aysgarth, where the school dominated the small village, he'd started to become cold inside. The nearer they got to the school, the more the cold clenched in his stomach, spreading outwards into his kidneys and down to his bladder.

'You'll be all right once we get there,' his Mother had said, but they both knew she was lying. When the car stopped and his trunk was collected by the porter he'd said 'Goodbye' formally, turned and walked away without a backward glance. He'd known there was nothing she could do. The cold had never really gone away that whole Michaelmas term. It was only back at home during the Christmas holiday that he'd been able to relax. 'I'm cold,' he'd say, and his mother would say, 'Come here darling,' and he'd snuggle up against her, putting his arms round her waist and burying his head into her body, and she would murmur, 'There, there,' and wrap her arms around him and stroke his hair.

'What did you do with the blanket?' he says. 'It's probably on the floor under your knitting.'

'You'll come in with me won't you, Godfrey?'

'Of course I will.'

He remembered she'd wanted him to come in when they'd gone to see the Doctor. It hadn't been the easiest of meetings. The Doctor had explained that if the treatment was unsuccessful in slowing the disease, then it would be only a matter of time before she became significantly more confused and it would be necessary to find a suitable clinic so she could die with dignity. The Doctor had explained the legislation passed in parliament last year which would make this possible. Godfrey thought how quickly the private sector had taken advantage of the business opportunity. So many care-homes had expanded their services, many offering comprehensive all-in-one packages, the care-home, the hospice, the clinic, the morgue and the burial or cremation at an all-inclusive price. It was on the extras where they made their money, he mused, the in-room media, the phone, non-thermogenic make-up, pearlescent white coffins.

And now here they are, on their final journey. He swings the car into the driveway and parks near the main entrance. Two nurses emerge even before the car comes to a halt on the faux marble tiles. One nurse, efficient in her dove grey uniform, opens the passenger door and helps his mother out. He goes into the office and hands over the necessary paperwork. He signs the forms in front of the receptionist who acts as the witness.

'Have you said "Goodbye" already?' she asks, matter of fact.

'No, I promised her I'd come in with her.' He catches the brief uncertainty in the receptionist's expression. She's wondering if we're going to change our minds, he thinks, but this was all decided months ago.

'That will be nice for her,' she says. 'It's always best if they have someone to hold their hand. You'd be surprised the number of people who don't.'

'How long does it usually take?' he asks.

'It's only a matter of minutes really, until they're sedated,' she says. 'They don't know anything after that. Will you be here tomorrow for the cremation?'

'It's ten o'clock isn't it. Yes, I'll be staying overnight at The Grand.'

It's turned out to be a wise precaution. He wants to be somewhere close by, but on his own.

One of the nurses looks in at the door. 'She's all tucked up and ready for you,' she says. 'Would you like to come and say Goodbye?'

He follows her into the "Petunia Suite". He'd expected something clinical, but the room was very pretty with delicate flowery wallpaper, matching bed covers, a Louis

XVI style bedside cabinet with a Dartington water decanter, and a pastel blue shade at the window.

The nurse murmurs, 'I'll leave you two together,' and backs out of the room closing the door quietly behind her. He sits in the French cottage style needlepoint chair beside the bed. His mother is wearing her best nightgown, a sheer apricot rayon fabric with embroidered blue flowers around the neck. Her make-up is still immaculate. She lies on her side, her mouth partly open, her breathing shallow, her eyes half closed. She extends a hand towards him.

'I'm cold,' she says.

He takes her hand in both of his. 'There, there,' he says, then sits in silence watching her eyes closing, feeling her hand slackening and becoming still. 'You'll be all right soon.'

DOUBTS AND BENEFITS

The first snowfall came the day before the real blizzard, like a scouting party ahead of an army. The date was memorable: December 7th 2011, the fifteenth anniversary of poor Will's passing. The date we never talk about but never forget. Just like that day the snow never stopped. The forecast was for more to come. I decided to walk down into the village to buy some emergency provisions. It was too risky to take the car. Chances were, even if it got down the hill all right, it wouldn't get back up again.

Edith had problems with her hips. One hip in particular was very painful and she had to walk with a stick. She worried terribly if I were out for too long.

'I don't want you going out in weather like this,' she said.

But I was insistent. 'I've got to go whilst I still can,' I said. 'If this snow gets much deeper, I'll not get down at all.'

'All right, John,' she said with a sigh. 'You go then. Are you going to wear your boots?'

'Of course I am, love. What did you think I was going to wear?'

'And you'll put on your ice-grips?'

'No, they won't fit over the boots.'

‘Well, you be careful,’ she said, hugging me round the chest and looking up into my face.

‘Don’t you go worrying about me, love,’ I said. I was so bundled up in my clothes that my arms wouldn’t hang against my sides.

‘Off you go then,’ she said, seeing me out the door, her hand on my back. ‘Take care.’

‘Close the door,’ I remember shouting. ‘You’ll be letting the cold in.’

The cottage was set back from the road with woods all around providing some shelter from the worst of the Pennine weather. Out on the road the snow was deeper than I’d expected and it was a bit of a struggle getting down the hill, especially where the road turned steeply down to the right and back again as you reached the bottom. By the time I’d made it to the village the wind had got up and the sides of the trees and chimney stacks were plastered white.

I did my best to get the snow off my boots before entering the shop, stamping my feet and kicking against the wall beside the entrance. There was a harsh buzzing noise as I pushed the door open. It used to have a little bell, I remembered, when it was the village Post Office and Edith worked there. They sold fresh cheese wrapped in greaseproof and bottled milk from Mike Kendall’s farm. The countertops were wooden. Edith had worked there for years, ever since the school closed in 1990 and her teaching days were ended. But the old Postmaster had retired a few years later and it had since been rebranded ‘Virgin Village.’ There was a Virgin Money “bank” where the old Post Office counter used to be. Edith had reached retirement age and it was clear the new owners didn’t value her experience. It was impossible for her to get another job, just as it had been for me when the mill was shut down.

The new manager, David Powter, was from Birmingham.

He had a heavy midlands accent which didn't fit around here and spoke through his nose. He was obsequious and over-familiar. I couldn't bring myself to like him. He was always trying to sell you things you didn't want, mobile phone packages, pay-for TV channels, life insurance, cut-price chocolate. He hired a seventeen-year-old girl part-time in Edith's place; the lass couldn't work out the change without a calculator.

'Mr. Webster, I didn't expect to see you down here today.' Powter stood by the counter polishing the Perspex cover over the display.

'It takes more than a few flakes of snow to keep me at home, Mr. Powter.'

I picked up a basket and made my purchases as quickly as I could – bread, margarine, eggs, cheese, tinned fish, beans, milk, tea.

'Do you want any cash out before I lock up behind the counter?'

'No, thank you. I'll be off. Mrs Webster will be wanting to get the kettle on.'

I left the shop, pulling on my gloves and bending my head into the wind with the snow coming heavier now. It was already getting dark. An old Ford Escort drew up just past me and parked half up on the pavement; I had to go out into the road to get past it, my boots crunching through the tyre tracks. I watched the driver get out. He looked to be in his late teens or early twenties, gangly, a fresh face with deep set eyes and long eyebrows which met in the middle. He was wearing a black leather jacket, dark trousers and surprisingly shiny black shoes. Not the sort of footwear for winter.

I had to lean forwards against the weather as I left the village. A bitter wind was starting to whip around the houses and the snow was weaving spirals of white in and out of the trees. I was weighed down by my shopping and dragged my legs through the drifts now forming across the road. The snow was halfway up my boots in places and my feet were getting heavier with every step.

I was halfway up the hill when I heard the car. It had rounded the first bend and I could hear the engine whining as the driver accelerated up the slope. I moved up onto the verge out of the way, my feet sinking through the icy crust into the long grass. As the car passed me it was already straining to maintain momentum. I could hear the crumpling of the snow under the tyres. When it reached the next bend there was a tearing noise as the tyres lost their grip. I raised a hand to shield my eyes as I squinted through the snow. The car was still moving, but slowly in a crablike fashion. The wheels were spinning and the rear was sliding round pointing the car diagonally across the road. The tyres suddenly regained their grip and the car shot forward across the opposite verge and turned over into the ditch.

I stumbled up the road. Other than a faint hissing noise coming from underneath the car there was no other sound at first. Everything was deadened by the snow. I walked with some difficulty to where the car had gone over. It had slid sideways down the steep bank and lay at an angle with the driver's side underneath. Snow was already covering the windows but I could see someone moving around inside.

Leaving the shopping by the roadside I half climbed, half slid, down the bank, leaning on the side of the car for support. All the time I sensed danger. There was a smell of petrol, burning rubber, a loud ticking noise. Fortunately, the engine had stalled but the ignition was still on, one of the headlights glowing beneath the ridge of snow piled in front of it and the wipers juddering across the windscreen. I reached the front passenger door but didn't have the strength to heave it open. I looked for something I could use to break the window but all was hidden by the snow. Then I saw a figure inside, a young lad by the look of him. He was struggling to push up towards the passenger door with his feet braced against the inside of the driver's door. Between the two of us, me pulling and the lad pushing up from below, we got the passenger door open enough for me to help pull him out. We fell together into the ditch in a tangle of arms and legs. I lay winded on my back in the snow for a few seconds, and worried there was no sound from the driver, but then I heard him coughing. His arms found mine again, and we struggled back to our feet and up the bank, hanging onto each other for support.

'Are you all right, lad?' I asked. 'Not injured are you?' I had hold of him by the shoulders and scanned his face in the fading light. I was pretty sure he was the person who'd parked beside the shop as I was leaving. He was very pale, his eyes like dull grey stones in his thin face. He had a cut on his forehead, a smudge of blood down the side of his cheek. He was trembling, whether with cold or shock, it wasn't clear.

'Are you hurt?' I asked again. He shook his head, dazed. Snow was settling in his hair. He was wearing gloves, but no coat.

'Have you got a coat?'

'N-no.' He shook his head again.

There was no prospect of getting help, no other traffic, no mobile signal.

'I live just up the road,' I said. 'You'd best come with me. We'll get you warm and dry indoors and then see what to do.' I saw the hesitation on his face. 'You'll catch your death out here.'

He was staring at me as if suddenly aware of what had happened.

'I've got s-s-stuff in the car,' he said.

'Can't it wait, lad? We've got to get inside and out of this weather.'

'No.' He was adamant, distracted. 'I c-can't leave my s-s-s-stuff.'

He started to shuffle back down the bank.

'Stop,' I shouted as he was trying to pull himself upright beside the rear bumper, 'Let me help.' The car had slid down the ditch nose first and the rear end was up in the air. The boot lid had come ajar. He was straining to prise it open further but was weak with shock, or perhaps concussion. There was something desperate about his movements.

'Just wait will you,' I urged him. So I slid back down the bank and pulled the boot lid up. There was a leather holdall inside, surprisingly heavy. He didn't want me to take it but was in no state to handle it himself. He was barely able to get back up the bank. He stopped half-way, holding onto a tree root and I passed the holdall to him so he could hang onto it whilst I clambered up beside him. The slope was gentler above and we managed to repeat the manoeuvre. Finally, we regained the roadside.

'So far, so good,' I said. I extended my hand. 'John Webster.'

'Darren.' He ducked his head.

I took another look at him. He was still trembling. He was taller than me, about 6' and lanky. With his black cropped hair, dark clothing and a hangdog expression, he looked like a teenage undertaker.

'Can you walk OK, do you think?'

'Yeah.'

'With that bag?'

'Yeah. I'm OK.'

'Right then.' I picked up my shopping bags from the roadside and together we pushed our way against the wind and the stinging snow up the hill to the cottage. As we reached the gate the front door opened and Edith hobbled out, one hand clutching her stick and the other raised like an antenna.

'Whatever's happened? I've been waiting and waiting. You've worried me to death.' She grabbed me around the shoulders. I could see tears in her eyes. She hung onto me as we stumbled into the house.

'Thank you, thank you,' she said to Darren as he followed us in. 'Had he fallen over? Where did you find him?'

Darren looked at her, lost for a response.

Without waiting for an answer, she sat me down on a kitchen chair, melting snow dripping onto the floor tiles, pools of water spreading out from under my boots. 'Where are you hurt?' she asked. Her hands explored me, touching my cheek, my shoulders, her eyes following, searching for injury. She looked down at my soaked trousers and snow-caked boots.

'Let's get them off first.' She kneeled with an effort. She looked round at Darren. 'I'm sorry. I don't know your name.'

'D-Darren,' he said, and ducked his head in this funny way he had, as if avoiding an arrow or a snowball.

'I'm all right, really, Edith,' I said. 'It's Darren who's hurt himself. He's been in an accident.'

'An accident?' Edith's voice rose sharply.

'His car's slid off the road. It's in the ditch.' I looked at Darren. 'I had to help you out, didn't I?'

Edith stared at me from fifteen years ago, her eyes wide with fright. I kept talking. 'It's a good job I saw it happen,' I said. 'I doubt there'll be anyone else coming up that hill tonight.'

'Nor down it,' said Edith, her face still troubled. 'It'll be worse up on the moor.'

'Looks like you'll have to stay here the night then, Darren.' I held up my hand to wave away any objections.

'Don't you worry. We've got a spare room, and enough food to keep us going for a day or two.' I nodded towards the shopping bags on the kitchen table.

Darren's eyes darted around the kitchen as if seeking a means of escape. He was frowning, his dark eyebrows plunging downwards to meet in the centre just above his eyes, one damp foot tapping spasmodically on the floor.

'Look, is there anyone you want to call? Is there anyone expecting you?'

He shook his head.

'So where were you heading. Were you on your way home?'

There was a pause before Darren replied. 'Yeah, I l-live in Darlington.'

'You've a fair way to go then. Well, we'll have to see what it looks like in the morning.'

Edith said something about a cup of tea and then going upstairs to make up a bed. She handed Darren a pair of thick socks. You'd best take off those wet shoes and socks,' she said. 'You can put these on for now.'

Darren sat with the socks in his hands looking like a patient outside a Doctor's waiting room. I tried to reassure him.

'You'll be all right here, Darren,' I said when Edith had gone upstairs. I could hear her moving about, the floorboards creaking, cupboards being opened and closed, a tap running in a basin. 'When Edith's finished you can go up and unpack your things.'

He looked at me blankly.

'Your luggage, lad. Have you got everything you need?'

Darren still looked uncertain.

'Like your washing things and pyjamas and that.'

'Oh no, Mr W-Webster.'

'John, call me John.'

'Oh, John then, no. I've got nothing like that.' He reached

down and grasped the handles of the holdall, and half-slid it under the table, as if to hide it from me. 'This is just my work stuff.'

'Sorry, lad, I misunderstood. So, you'll need some overnight things then? That's all right. I'm sure we'll have everything you'll be wanting.'

'Thanks, Mr W-Webster, s-sorry, John.'

I went out to the foot of the stairs and shouted up. 'Edith, Darren'll need some overnight things.'

His leather jacket was on the chair back and he leaned over and pulled his mobile out of a pocket. 'Can I charge my phone?'

I pointed to a socket at the corner of the worktop. 'You can plug it in there, but it won't do you much good. There's no signal here.'

'No signal?' Darren was startled and switched his phone on and stared at the screen as if to conjure up a signal out of willpower. He looked up like a child having a toy taken away from him.

'Never mind. You can use the landline.'

'What, in here?' Darren was breathing heavily and his fingers were pressed so hard on the table that his knuckles were white.

'Not if you don't want. There's an extension in the room upstairs.'

The tension was relieved by Edith, who came down at that point and heard the end of the conversation. She was struggling with her arms full of clothes.

'The phone's not working,' she said. 'I meant to tell you earlier but I forgot. The line must be down again.' She looked at Darren, eyebrows raised. 'So, you're properly stuck, aren't you Darren,' she said brightly. 'Well, look what I've got for you.' She spread the items out on the kitchen table like she'd been shopping for Christmas presents. 'Here's a pullover in case you're cold this evening, and a clean shirt for the morning, and a clean set of underwear and some slippers – they're unused. There's a dressing gown and some towels on the bed and a flannel.'

Darren looked bemused, unsure what to say. He was like a dog caught in a trap, eyes darting everywhere. Edith just went on, plucking at his arm and saying, 'You're feeling a bit shaky, I know. You stay put and drink your tea, then I'll show you your room and the bathroom. We've got a spare razor and shaving soap and a toothbrush, and…'

I saw Darren starting to stare with increasing confusion. 'You're about the same height and build as our son, William,' I said. 'You were wondering how come we'd so many things that'd fit you, weren't you?'

'Yeah.' Darren gave a nervous laugh. 'He won't mind?'

'He won't mind, lad. Don't you worry.'

'But is he around? When will he be b-back?'

I could feel Edith looking at me. 'He won't be back, lad.'

'Drink up your tea,' she said, 'and we'll show you to your room.'

'Up the wooden stairs,' said Edith cheerfully as we all went up, me leading the way, Darren behind me hanging onto his holdall, and Edith bringing up the rear, stumbling with her arms full of clothes.

I saw the look of surprise on Darren's face as we pushed through the bedroom door. He took it all in. On the wall beside the bed were posters of the earth from space, fighter aircraft, Eminem. The shelves on the opposite wall were packed with books, engineering and flying manuals, children's books, *Where the Wild Things Are*, and beside the bed, *The Curious Incident of the Dog in the Night-Time*. It had a bookmark sticking out between pages 68 and 69. There was a washbasin with a mirror, glass shelves above and a vanity unit below, Lynx Deodorant and Jean Paul Gaultier aftershave on the shelves. Beside the wardrobe were running shoes and walking boots.

Darren looked like a rescue dog in a new house, nervously inspecting each corner, sniffing at the furnishings. 'I won't touch anything,' he said.

'No, no lad. You go ahead,' I said, patting him on the back. 'Treat it like it's your own. We want you to feel comfortable.'

'Well, just tonight.'

'We'll have to see,' I said. 'The forecast's no better tomorrow. Anyway, you make yourself at home and come down when you're ready. We'll have dinner about seven o'clock, I expect.'

He didn't come down until just before seven and stood very quietly by the door to the dining room.

'Come in lad, and sit yourself down,' I said.

He did so, saying, 'Is here all right,' with his hand on a chair. He looked pale and his eyes were everywhere except looking at us. He sat down and inspected his hands. They were beautiful hands, with long tapered fingers and immaculate fingernails so shiny they looked as if they had been lacquered.

'I don't want anything to eat,' he said.

'Don't you feel very well?' said Edith. 'I've made some chicken soup, and then there's sausages and mashed potatoes.'

He just stared at the tablecloth.

'I expect you're still a bit shaken,' Edith went on. 'A bit of soup'll do you good.'

'Just the soup then, thanks.'

We ate in near silence.

When we'd finished Darren said, 'I think I'll go back to b-bed, if you don't mind, Mrs Webster.'

'Of course,' said Edith. 'Are you sure you're all right? Is there anything we can get you? Have you got a headache?'

He didn't want anything but got up and went quietly back up the stairs.

The following morning the snow was thicker than ever, more like a duvet than a blanket. Nothing moved. There was no sound. Edith sat in the kitchen listening to the local radio.

'They've closed the A66,' she said, as I came downstairs and picked up the waiting cup of tea. 'There'll be no road open over the moor.'

'It looks like Darren won't be going anywhere today then.'

'Oh, and you'd not credit it, but David Powter was robbed yesterday.'

'Powter? What do you mean? How do you know?'

'It was on the radio. They said the Virgin shop in Aysgarth. It must be him.'

'What happened? Did they say what happened?'

'Not really. Only that it happened at closing time. They said the shopkeeper was attacked.'

'It must have been just after I left,' I said, bewildered. 'He was closing the shop then. He asked if I wanted any cash before he locked up behind the counter.'

We looked at each other. I felt a nameless anxiety.

'Darren's not down yet,' said Edith.

'And?'

'It couldn't have been him, could it?'

I wanted this conversation to stop before it went any further, but the thought had been voiced and couldn't be unsaid. 'I suppose it could have been. He drew up beside the shop as I was leaving. It was only ten minutes or so later that he passed me on the road. But he's a nice lad; surely he wouldn't have robbed the shop. He doesn't seem the type.'

'He's very nervous. I can't imagine him attacking anyone.'

'I wonder how badly Powter was hurt.'

Edith looked up at the ceiling. We heard the floorboards creaking above us. 'He'll be down any minute,' she whispered.

'I don't know why we're whispering,' I said, but I kept my voice down.

'I don't suppose the phone is working again? Have you tried it?'

'No, shall I try it now?'

'No, not in front of Darren,' I said. 'Let's wait.'

Shortly afterwards Darren came downstairs, wearing the same clothes as the day before. We both looked at the floor.

'Did you sleep well?' I asked finally.

'Yeah, OK, thank you,' said Darren. He looked red eyed and nervous. I knew full well that he'd been up half the night. I'd seen his light on under the door and heard him moving around. It had sounded as if he was packing.

'How are you feeling?'

'Oh, better, thanks.'

'The roads are all closed over the moor,' I said. 'We heard it on the radio.'

'But I can't just stay here,' said Darren.

'Well, you certainly can't go anywhere today,' I said.

Darren's eyes narrowed and his mouth tightened as he thought this through.

Edith butted in. 'You can't go out in this. The snow's drifted really bad. Look out the front.'

Darren looked. You couldn't even see the road, just a succession of white drifts enveloping the gateway and burying the hedge.

'How long before they clear the roads, do you know?'

'Well, they always clear the main roads first before they get around to us. It'll be two or three days I should think, so long as there's no more snow.'

Darren was contemplating the floor, biting his lower lip. Suddenly he looked up at me, bright-eyed and almost childlike in his eagerness. He said, 'I can pay for my keep. I can do stuff for you whilst I'm here, clear the snow and things.'

'There's no need to pay us, lad, but you can help clear the snow. We could do with the help,' I said, looking at Edith. She gave a little nod and a sideways glance in Darren's direction behind his back.

As soon as he'd gone upstairs after breakfast, we were back to whispering again.

'There's nowt we can do,' I said. 'We're cut off. Even if the phone line is restored, no-one can get here and we can't get out. We're best to keep quiet until we know we can get help.' Our eyes met; we were in this together.

'Well, you can't be sure it's him,' said Edith.

'Of course I'm not sure,' I said. 'But we can hardly ask him, can we. Meanwhile, we've just got to behave as if nothing's amiss.'

Later that morning there was another snowstorm, the wind whistling around the trees, the snow spinning in chaotic vortices. You couldn't go outside. We sat in the kitchen much of the time. Darren was fidgety with nothing to do. He kept getting up and wandering around. There were no newspapers; there was no phone. None of us, including Darren, could stomach daytime TV. Finally, Darren's wanderings took him into the utility room, to clean up the boots he'd been using and shine his shoes.

"Utility room" was a bit of a grand title; it was really a

lean-to built onto the side of the kitchen. In addition to the usual clutter, it had the portable generator, sitting on an old rug covered with oil stains and surrounded by assorted engine parts and my haphazard collection of spanners and wrenches.

I heard Darren's exclamation, and then, 'I see you've got an old SGS Diesel. A good precaution that up here, I should think.' It was the most I had heard him say since his arrival.

'Aye, there's rarely a winter goes by when we don't lose the power for a couple of days. Though it needs an overhaul; that's another of those jobs I should have got done before the snow came.'

'What's wrong with it?' he asked.

I tried to explain. 'It starts OK but it cuts out after a couple of minutes, and then it's a devil to start again.'

'I'll fix it for you if you like,' he said. 'They had one at the farm where I used to live. It's no problem.'

He was the happiest I'd seen him. He was meticulous, methodically removing bolts, washers, and plugs, and cleaning and oiling them before laying them out carefully in order on the mat.

'I can see you know what you're doing,' I said. 'You put me to shame.'

'It's not my trade, you understand,' he said, 'but I know my way round engines and electrics.'

He'd been very guarded about his background, but I risked a question.

'So, you lived on a farm, did you, Darren? Where was that then?'

'You wouldn't know it. Keadby: it's a little village near Scunthorpe. There's a big bridge over the Trent. We lived in a farm cottage.' He'd stood up, wiping his hands with a rag. 'It's all done. We can put some diesel in and see if she starts OK.'

I had to go to the shed to get the diesel. The opportunity for more questions had gone.

At dinnertime I tried again. Edith had made a beef casserole with roast potatoes and had put a big tray of Yorkshire puddings on the end of the table. She was busily pronging them with a fork and pushing them onto our plates. She gave three to Darren.

'You'll be hungry I expect,' she said. 'You had hardly anything to eat yesterday. You're feeling better, aren't you?'

'Yeah, much b-better, thanks.'

'Darren did a grand job repairing the generator,' I said.

'We're right grateful,' she said and gave a little smile.

'You were saying your Dad taught you?' I prompted.

'Step-Dad.' But then he hunched down and started to stutter.

'And what did your step-Dad do?'

'Hah! Nothing m-much. He was unemployed. He made a bit on the side fixing engines, agricultural equipment, TVs, audio, computers, all s-sorts of things. He was clever; the house was always full of stuff.'

'So, he had a repair business, did he?'

'Sort of, but his main business was cars, doing them up. There was a big garage at the corner of the lane and he used to help them out.' He had become more voluble again, more comfortable with us. He started looking at Edith rather than having his eyes cast down on the table. 'They had a sort of connection to the farm. They used one of the barns as a workshop.'

It sounded a bit dubious to me, but then Edith chipped in.

'What about your Mum?'

'Step-Mum. She was useless. She was an artist. Had a sort of studio out the back, never sold anything.'

He was becoming quite talkative between mouthfuls of Edith's Yorkshires, and I noticed he was stammering less.

'So, you were an orphan then?' said Edith.

'Yeah. Hull Seaman's Orphanage 'til I was five, then fostered.'

'No brothers or sisters?'

'No, only me. They wanted to foster more but... I dunno what happened.'

'You said you live in Darlington.'

'Yeah. I'm doing an I.T course. It'll finish next summer.'

Edith butted in, 'And you'll not be going back home afterwards?'

Darren shook his head slowly and deliberately, pursing his lips. 'I left home as soon as I turned eighteen. That was when the allowance ran out. They only ever fostered me to get the allowance.'

'So what do you want to do once you've got your qualifications?'

I was surprised by his answer: 'I want to work for a charity that helps people.'

I was nonplussed, dying to ask him to explain, but I didn't know what to say. There was an uneasy silence and I felt I'd pushed things far enough.

The next day the skies cleared, solid cerulean blue; the sun on the white landscape hurt your eyes. Darren spent all day either clearing snow or chopping wood. You could hear the steady clunk of the axe head followed by the clatter of the split logs. I wanted to help him, but Edith stopped me.

'John, love. Let him do it. It's something he can do to help.'

'Oh, all right. But I can't sit around doing nothing.'

'You can wash the floors in the kitchen and utility room

if you want something to do. All this snow getting tramped in all the time and you know I can't kneel with my hip.'

So, I cleaned the floors, wondering not for the first time how long Edith would have to wait for an operation.

'It's an elective procedure,' our doctor had explained. 'There are other people a lot worse off in the queue.'

'So, what have we paid our National Insurance Contributions for, all these years?'

'I'm sorry, John, there's nothing I can do.'

'Unless we go private.'

'Of course.'

'We've been betrayed, haven't we, the welfare state, the NHS free for all at the point of need.'

He sighed. We'd known each other for years. There was nothing I could say to him that he didn't know already.

The snowplough finally made it up the hill the following day, but left mountains of dirty frozen snow at the sides of the road. Darren was outside clearing the path. The light faded fast. I peeled vegetables for dinner whilst Edith sat at the table chopping dried fruits for a cake. She couldn't stand for too long because of her hip. The sound of the phone ringing was almost shocking, interrupting the silence. We looked at each other.

'Thank the Lord, the phone's back!' said Edith. She reached over to answer it. Her friend, Muriel, had called from the village to see if we were all right. She was bursting with news about the robbery at the shop.

Edith carried the phone to the table and sat down, bent over the receiver.

'No,' she said in a low voice, then, 'Ah-ha,' which she kept repeating every few seconds. One time she giggled and said, 'Silly old fool,' and another time, 'Serves him right,' and finally she said, 'You'll ring again if you get any more news, won't you?'

She put the phone down. Although it didn't register at the time, I realised later that she hadn't mentioned Darren once. 'Muriel says they found Powter unconscious, sat in a chair behind the banking counter. The safe door was open and all the cash had been taken, the drawers emptied, and the till in the shop.' She'd raised her eyebrows and was biting her lower lip as if to say, 'Who would credit it?'

'Was he hurt? Powter?' I asked. This seemed more important than anything else.

'No, not really.' Her eyes were wide. 'They called the doctor. It seems he was chloroformed or something. They think with some sort of spray.'

'Well I never.' I was starting to see the burglary in a different light. 'What else did Muriel say?'

She said Powter was just putting the banking cash in the safe when all the lights went out. He heard someone come up behind him and turned around but that's all he remembers.'

'Who found him?' I asked.

'Mr Partridge from down the road. He'd seen the lights were still on so he'd dashed across to get some milk before the shop shut. He went in but there was no-one there; then he saw the till open and went round the counter.'

'But didn't you say all the lights were out?'

'Yes, they were. But it seems the thief switched them on again when he left.'

I started to laugh. 'You've got to hand it to him.'

'Whatever do you mean?'

'Well, he slips in the back just on closing time, turns the electric off, so no lights. He chloroforms Powter and sits him all comfy in a chair. Everything's unlocked. He helps himself to all the cash, switches the electric back on when he leaves out the back, so someone'll notice summat's up pretty quick, and meanwhile he scarpers.'

‘And you think he scarpered up the hill and crashed his car?’

‘Maybe.’

‘And you rescued him.’

‘It’s looking more like it. Tell you what though. We’d best not say anything to Darren. Not yet at any road. We still don’t know for sure if he did it, and if he did, it’s best he doesn’t know what we know.’

We were standing in the lounge. Edith had turned and was looking out towards the road. I followed her gaze. Darren bent over a shovel digging out a path through the enormous ridge of snow left by the snowplough across the front of the garden.

‘He’s been out there since two o’clock,’ she said.

‘He’s a hard worker.’

‘I wonder how much he took from the shop.’ Edith looked crestfallen, her hands twisting in her lap.

‘I’m not so bothered so long as he didn’t hurt anyone.’

‘Muriel was clear about that: Powter wasn’t hurt, only his pride.’

Edith nodded, as if thinking how best to say what was coming next. ‘I can’t quite believe it, you know,’ she said. ‘If you hadn’t seen him at the shop then we would be none the wiser, would we? We’re the only people who can put two and two together.’

‘But we can’t be sure, can we? It could just be coincidence.’

‘Course, we could always have a look in his room.’ Edith had her head on one side squinting up at me, her forehead wrinkled into a question-mark.

‘You mean, have a look in that holdall of his?’

Edith nodded. I could hear the whine of the washing machine coming to the end of its spin-cycle. We both listened to it slowing down, waiting for the final “clunk” as it stopped.

‘And what if we find the evidence?’ I said.

'Well,' she said, biting her lip, 'he'll be gone soon won't he, when the road's open.'

'Do you want me to look now? It's a good time.'

'John, will you? I'll stay here, then I can call up and warn you if it looks like he's coming in.

So, I went upstairs.

It didn't take me long to find it. The holdall was just where I might have expected, under the bed. Even as I reached for it, I could tell it was empty, and I remembered hearing Darren creeping around the room on the first night. I'd thought it'd sounded as if he was packing, but unpacking seemed more like it. He must have been hiding away whatever was in the holdall, but where?

There weren't many places something could be hidden. I searched the wardrobe and then the drawers, one by one. I riffled through the folded shirts, the paired socks, the sports equipment. How many times must Edith have dusted and cleaned in here over the years? She must have done it in secret when I'd been out shopping or doing the garden. The room was a shrine we never visited together. Touching the shirts, feeling the collars, lifting a pile of engineering manuals and placing them back down again, I almost forgot what I was supposed to be doing. Eventually I came downstairs again.

'What did you find?' said Edith.

'I found the holdall under the bed but it's empty. Whatever was in it must be somewhere in that room, but I'm blowed if I know where.'

'Are you really sure it was full of, well, you know what?'

'Look, I don't know what was in it but whatever it was it isn't there now.'

Edith tugged at my arm. 'Darren's finished. He's coming up the path.'

Darren came round the side of the cottage and took his boots off in the back porch before coming in. 'It's all clear now,' he said. 'We'll be able to get down the hill on the road. I suppose I'll be able to get a bus from the village tomorrow.'

'And the phone's back on,' I said. 'I'll phone the bus company and find out when they're running. Oh, and Darren, do you want to make any phone calls? Your friends must be wondering what's happened to you.'

Darren frowned. 'I'll ring them later if that's OK.'

I called the bus company.

'They'll run a bus tomorrow. They say to check in the morning,' I said to Darren.

'So, you'll be here tonight,' said Edith.

There was an uncomfortable silence before Darren said, 'Thanks ever so for putting me up.' He paused and coloured before adding, 'You're good people. I'd like to help you more.'

'Well, we've enjoyed having you,' said Edith. 'Haven't we, John?'

'Aye, and you've been very helpful while you've been here.'

'Tell you what,' said Darren. 'You're very low on everything, aren't you? Would you like me to go with you down the shop? I could help carry it back.'

'Oh, that would be a real help,' said Edith.

I shook my head at her over Darren's shoulder. I was puzzled. If Darren had carried out the robbery, then he must be very confident he would not be recognised. But if he went with me to the shop and was recognised then we could all be implicated in the crime. Maybe he really was innocent. Anyway, I could see that Edith was much more concerned about me going down to the village on my own in bad weather. 'Yes, you go, the both of you,' she said, staring me down. 'I'll make a list.'

I wondered about Darren's motivation. He was always looking for opportunities to help us. Was he just being thoughtful? Or did he want to find out what was known about the robbery? It seemed a bit risky to me. And how would I introduce him? I didn't want to say anything about Darren if I could help it. I realised we had already crossed a line, Edith and me. The phone was back. We could have rung the police with our suspicions. Edith could have mentioned something to Muriel. We hadn't even mentioned anything about the robbery to Darren. We'd each of us come to the same conclusion. The truth was obvious but we didn't want to know it. What we didn't know we couldn't tell.

As we set off down the hill with a pile of bags and Edith's shopping list in my trouser pocket, I said, 'Darren. When we go into the shop, I'll have to say something about who you are. The manager, Powter, is certain to ask.'

'Perhaps it's b-better I don't come in.'

How much did Darren think I knew? There was a lot that remained unspoken.

'No, you know what village folk are like. All the curtains'll be twitching. And Powter's an old busybody. I can't stand him myself. No, you'll have to come in and if necessary, I'll just say you were visiting and got trapped by the snow. Okay?'

'Okay.'

We hung onto each other as we picked our way in the fading light down the tracks left by the plough, me placing one foot gingerly in front of the other, shopping bags in one hand, the other grasping Darren by the elbow, him sometimes going first and letting me lean on him. Halfway down we came to the spot where Darren's car had gone into the ditch. As I'd expected, it was buried deep under the embankment of snow.

‘What’ll you do about the car? It’ll be ages before anyone can get it out of the ditch.’

‘I don’t know,’ said Darren. ‘At least it’s off the road. I mean it won’t cause an obstruction or anything.’

‘Old Mike Kendall, the farmer up the road,’ I said. ‘He’ll get it out for you once the snow is cleared. But it’ll need repairing I expect?

‘Dunno,’ said Darren. ‘Maybe not.’

‘Don’t you think you should report it to the police?’ I wanted to see his reaction, but he was guarded.

‘I dunno. There’s no-one was injured.’

I let it pass.

‘Mr Webster,’ Powter hailed me even before the door had closed behind us, the buzzer still sounding. He rubbed his hands. His voice was like dripping. ‘How are you? How have you coped with all this snow? This’ll be the first time you’ve got out, I should imagine.’

I could tell he was aching to tell his story.

‘Yes, it is,’ I replied. ‘We’ve had some help as it turns out. Darren here was visiting and got trapped by the snow. So, he’s been helping clear the paths and all sorts. Anyway, from what we’ve heard you’ve got a bit of a tale to tell.’

‘I should say so. I hardly know where to begin.’

And so the story was retold between purchases of bread and milk, kitchen rolls and washing powder, a long list ticked off by Powter as we talked.

‘So, you remember hardly anything about it,’ I said. ‘You never saw the thief?’

‘No, I couldn’t tell you anything about him.’

‘What about your CCTV camera?’

‘No good at all. It runs on the battery if the power goes off, but it’s fixed over the counter and I reckon the thief had one of them lantern torches that you can angle upwards. He just pointed it at the camera. All you can see is a white blur. And he must have been wearing one of them head torches, you know, they're on a band round your forehead. You can see it moving around when he was emptying the safe.'

'And the police have no clue at all?'

'No. He was wearing gloves. He never spoke, not that I heard anyway.' Powter gave a sharp hurt bark of a laugh. 'The only thing we know about him, the only clue we got from the CCTV, is that he had very shiny shoes.'

'You're joking.'

'No, you could see the torchlight reflected off them as he moved around. That's all we know.' He put on an official sounding voice. 'The police are looking for a man with shiny shoes.'

I couldn't speak. I didn't know where to look. It took an immense effort not to look down at Darren's feet, even though I knew he was wearing wellingtons.

'How did he get away?'

'We don't know that either. Though I'll tell you what.' He leaned forward over the counter, his face nearly in mine. 'It happened that afternoon with all the snow, right after you'd been in. It looks like a car may have drawn up outside just as you left, Mr Webster, so you may have seen it. In fact, the police will be round if they haven't already. They think if that was him, he probably drove up the hill after leaving the shop and could have gone past you and over the moor. He'd have been lucky not to get stuck in the snow. Did you see a car when you left the shop?'

Darren was beside me packing the shopping into the bags. It was like standing next to a halogen heater. I shuffled slightly away from him and screwed up my face looking straight back at Powter. 'Now you mention it, I think someone did draw up behind me as I left the shop. I remember thinking they were only just in time if they wanted something before you closed, but I didn't get a look at them.'

'And did anyone pass you on the hill?' He had this habit of looking down his nose at you. I don't think he was sneering, but it looked like it. He was doing it now.

I thought again. 'I can't say. All I remember was the snow. It came down so fast I was lucky to get home.'

'Thanks, Mr Webster,' said Darren as we walked back up the hill. It was more difficult now, weighed down with the shopping, but Darren had two big bags in his left hand, and another over his shoulder, leaving his spare hand to help keep me steady. There was just the two of us on the road, like Mole and Ratty, dwarfed by the trees on either side, our footprints in the snow tracing the memory of how far we'd come.

'Thanks for what, lad?' I said, knowing perfectly well.

'Th-thanks for not saying anything about the car.'

We'd both stopped. I wanted to see his eyes. We had to understand each other. We'd already crossed one line back in the cottage. Here was another.

'Look, lad, I don't rightly know why I didn't say anything. Perhaps it's because I don't know anything for certain, and I don't want to be the one who sets the police on your tail.' I said this while hanging onto his arm like we were tied together. 'But I'm afraid they'll want a word with you soon enough once they find the car.'

'What makes you think that, Mr Webster?'

'Well, it is your car, isn't it?' I looked up at Darren, a new thought jumping to the surface.

'No, it's not.'

'Well, whose is it then?' I stopped and tugged on Darren's arm and looked into his face.

'I d-don't know, Mr Webster.'

'You mean it's stolen?'

'Sort of. More borrowed, if you like. If it hadn't been for the snow, it would have been parked back near where it was left, no harm done.'

I felt myself sinking slowly into a delicious conspiracy, like watching a conjuror and acknowledging the sleight of hand but allowing myself to believe the magic. 'Won't there be evidence? Fingerprints?' Another glance at Darren's face gave me the answer. 'No? You'd have worn gloves of course. But would you have left anything in it?'

'Nothing, Mr Webster. Nothing at all, I'm always very careful with things like that.'

I didn't know what to say.

As we approached the cottage, I said. 'It's best we don't mention this to Mrs Webster at the moment, Darren. Leave it to me. I'll tell her in my own good time.'

But even as we were unloading the shopping on the kitchen worktop, inhaling the smell of baking, seeing the table with its blue check tablecloth laid for dinner, Edith turned round from the oven and wiped her hands on her apron.

'The police were here, John. I told them you'd gone to the shop. They want to speak to you about the robbery. They think you may have seen something. They didn't want to wait. They said they'd be back.'

'Did they now? What did they ask you? Just so I can get my story straight.'

'Well, they asked if we'd seen anything when you'd come back from the shop. I didn't tell them anything really. I just said I was sorry I couldn't help them.'

We were both looking intently at Edith. Darren shifted from one foot to the other, chewing on his bottom lip.

'You're thinking about Darren, aren't you?' Edith went on. 'You're thinking, did I tell them about Darren?'

'Well, yes. Did you?'

'No. It's none of their business who we have to stay. Anyway,' she said, looking at me. 'What did you tell Powter? I suppose Darren went into the shop with you?'

'Aye, he did.' I hesitated. 'I told him he was visiting, that he's been trapped by the snow.'

All this time we'd been staring at each other. Darren had stood there, mute, beside the shopping. Now we both looked at him.

'I d-don't know w-w-w-what to s-s-say.' Darren's eyes were cast down. He'd ducked his head and he was fiddling with one of the shopping bags. 'Y-you took me in. Y-you never said owt. You've known all along?'

'We don't know anything, lad,' I said, my voice as sharp and firm as I could make it. 'We took you in because of the snow. We liked you.' I looked across at Edith. 'We both like you, don't we, Edith?'

I could see Edith was struggling. She swallowed hard. 'You remind us a bit of our William,' she said, her eyes brimming with tears. 'There, I've said it now. He would have been about your age when he died.'

It was the unspoken fault line between us. We never talked about William's death. Edith still cleaned his bedroom. William's boots were still in the rack in the utility room. The bookmark was still in-between pages 68 and 69 of *The Curious Incident of the Dog in the Night-Time*.

'I'm really sorry, Mrs Webster. I did wonder if he'd died, just from some of the things in his room.'

'He died in a car accident,' Edith went on. 'He was at university in Durham. He was coming home for Christmas. A friend gave him a lift. The weather was bad coming over the moor…' Her voice trailed away. She sat down at the kitchen table and began to cry silently, her shoulders heaving. I couldn't bear it. We had suffered the same sorrow for so long without sharing it. I moved across to her, held her close, her head on my chest, my arms round her. I looked round at Darren over my shoulder.

'You can stay here if you like,' I blurted out. 'Treat it a bit like home. You could come for weekends and holidays, and for Christmas. We'd like that, wouldn't we, Edith?'

She opened her eyes, blinking, looking at him. 'Please say "yes", Darren,' she said.

I cleared my throat and looked at the floor. 'We're not condoning what you've done, Darren, but we don't think you're a bad lot. There's those who've done a lot worse and got away with it. Bankers. Lawyers. Politicians.'

Darren didn't respond at first, another one of his silences. Then, 'If I did stay,' he said, 'I think there'd be ways I could help you.'

'I'm sure you could,' I said. 'But don't you worry about that. Is that settled then? You'll move into the room upstairs. We can change the room around if you want to bring some of your stuff over. When the weather clears, that is.'

'This calls for a celebration,' said Edith. 'I'll put the kettle on.'

Christmas was celebrated in style that year. The fact that the champagne came from Virgin Village and was almost certainly paid for with cash from their own till made it all the sweeter.

After the Christmas holidays Darren returned to Darlington to complete his I.T. course. At least that bit of what he'd told us was true. During the following year he came to stay during the holidays and made a number of trips around the country, not that he told us much about them, just that it was part-time work which paid for his computer course. I didn't care to ask any more, but each time he was away I worried about him.

It was during the long hot summer that year when Edith's arthritic hip became worse. She was in a lot a pain and had great difficulty with the stairs. Darren said she should go private.

'Don't be daft, Darren,' I said. 'How do you suppose we could afford that?'

'How much would you say it would cost, Mr Webster?'

'Good Lord, I don't know, upwards of £15,000.'

He ducked his head, squinted up at me. 'That's what I thought. You should let me pay for it, Mr Webster.' He always reverted to Mr Webster when he was serious.

'And where would you be able to get your hands on that kind of money?' I knew the answer to the question, and I also knew what he would say.

'It's best we don't talk about that. It's all in cash of course, but we could open some new bank accounts so it wouldn't be queried.'

What to say. I loved Edith dearly and couldn't bear to see her suffering. And we had both taken Darren to our hearts, averting our eyes from his part-time "work", so I just asked, 'And where is the money now, Darren?'

He had a peculiar expression on his face, part sadness, as if seeking forgiveness. 'It's in the garden,' he said, and hurriedly added, 'but you won't be able to find it, and no-one else will.'

So, I talked to Edith, and got an appointment to see the doctor. We went together.

'You know, Doctor, when we talked about a hip replacement last time you said there was a long waiting list.'

'I'm sorry, John, but you know how it is.'

'Yes, I do, and you said about going private.'

‘It’s a lot of money, John.’

‘Well, we’ve decided to do it. To go private, I mean. As a matter of fact, we’ve had a bit of a windfall.’

It was when Edith needed a second hip operation the following year that I decided to take a more active role in Darren’s affairs. After all, by then I was complicit. So, we bought a car, a Volvo estate, and whenever Darren went on one of his trips – always after a great deal of research – I would drive him to near wherever he had decided to “borrow” a car. I then followed him to a rendezvous close to wherever another unworthy shop was about to be relieved of its takings. The proceeds would be transferred to my car whilst Darren drove the “borrowed” car back to the spot from which it had been taken. I would pick Darren up from round the corner and we would return home. Edith’s vegetable plot became the storage place for the cash. It was wrapped in plastic hidden twelve inches down under the trenches between the crops. We transferred it in small amounts to a growing number of different banks, all in time for Edith’s second hip operation.

All that was two years ago. Darren finished his I.T. course and moved in to stay with us permanently. We make a good team. Our next project is to re-start the travelling library which used to run up the dale and back every Friday, and after that we hope to re-furbish the village hall. Longer term we hope to raise the funds needed to re-open the primary school in the village, and after that, well, who knows?

SNIP, SNIP

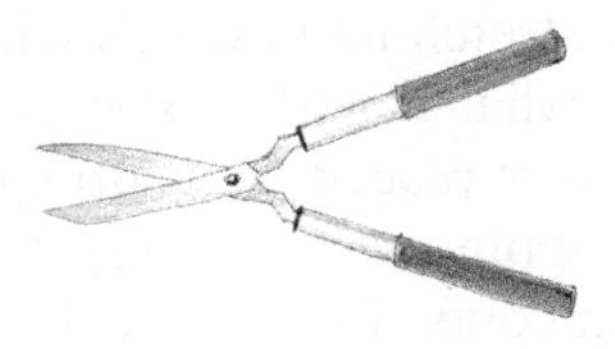

I stood on the terrace in my pyjamas looking down at the gardener. He plodded round the edge of the pool and across the lawn below me carrying an old wooden pair of steps which he put up beside a large oleander. He was a dear old man, Alfonso, employed by the Edifico Regal for over twenty years. Not a word of English mind you, which didn't endear him to us ex-pats.

He didn't help himself either, making up for his lack of language skills with obsequiousness. He showed willing by nodding a lot and was always ready with a 'Buenos' and a smile whether or not it was appropriate to the occasion. You only had to say 'Hola, Alfonso' and no matter what he was doing he was pre-programmed to respond 'Buenos, com' esta?' A nod, a wide smile through crooked teeth, eyes squinting in the bright Mediterranean light.

I returned to my sunbed, my morning coffee (it was too early for alcohol) and my newspaper. The contents were depressing. A swarm of migrants was spreading across Europe, none making it to this island, thank God, a stock market crash in China. I turned to the sports pages.

Snip snip, went Alfonso's shears in the background.

England had beaten San Marino, Andy Murray had lost to Federer.

Snip, snip, I drifted.

When I next stirred myself to look down over the balustrade Alfonso had almost finished pruning the Oleander, with only the topmost branches needing to be trimmed. He was standing precariously on the narrow wooden platform at the apex of the steps, stretching upwards with the shears in his hands. I thought, what would happen if he slipped? What if, say, the steps were placed on a soft spot in the lawn and they gave way, tipping over to one side? Or if he was distracted by someone. Even now I could see he was stretching up, leaning over to his right, almost on tiptoe. Snip, snip. And what if his foot slipped and as his arms windmilled to keep his balance he dropped the shears so they fell first, handles landing on the grass with the blades briefly pointing upwards, open, like the jaws of a crocodile. And what if the gardener followed them down to earth, his body landing on top of the shears, the blades skewering his back?

Snip, snip.

'Alfonso?' I called. 'Hola, Alfonso. Com' esta?'

He twisted around, turned his head, smiling, almost nodding in that strange way he had, opened his mouth to respond, and slipped.

Long Listed in Fish Flash Fiction Competition, 2016

THE LODGER

She should never have put an ad in the paper. She knew that now. But the college had inspected the property, found it wanting and withdrawn it from their lists. Anyway, she thought she might do better on her own; she could be choosier and the rent would be paid in cash.

And Colm was the lodger from heaven. In his mid-thirties he was older than the students she had been used to, and he was Irish, but no matter. He paid cash in advance, didn't complain about the room, didn't mind the cats, kept himself to himself, and was always polite, even deferential. And he had become so useful.

'Well now, Mrs Betteridge, how do you think you'd be doing with this?' He'd just got in and was holding a metal pole with a handle at one end and a claw on the other. 'It extends, d'you see? And then you can reach up like this.' He reaches the claw up to the top shelf in the kitchen, and brings it down again clamped to a tin of peace slices. 'Or, if you drop somethin', like your cigarettes,' and he puts her cigarette packet on the ground, 'you can reach down and pick it up again.' He smiles broadly. 'Isn't that marvellous now?' It's one of several items which he's brought from the

Mobility Shop on his way back from work. 'It's a ten pounds deposit that I paid, but I can take it back if you don't want it.'

She never discovered precisely where he worked. 'Oh, it's an office I work at in town,' he would say, 'but I can choose my own hours, you know.' In fact, he was often back at odd times during the day and some days never went to work at all.

She picked up the device and opened and closed the claw.

'Oh, Colm, bless you, it looks wonderful. It's very sweet of you. Here, let me pay you.' She limped over to the table leaning on her stick.

'It's no trouble at all, Mrs. Betteridge. Now you sit down by the window and I'll get you a glass of the good stuff.'

Helen usually had a small glass of the good stuff in the evenings, to help her sleep, but Colm allowed her a treat sometimes during the day.

It was only a couple of months since Colm moved in but already Helen felt it was like having a real man about the house for the first time since being on her own. Not that Colm reminded her of her husband; Terry had been a big handsome man with a red face and beefy hands, affable and generous. Colm was more like a weasel, but he had the same ability to command. There was a sureness about him, as if he always knew what he was doing.

After Terry had passed away, she had realised that all their friends were really his friends, not hers. She had no family living and gradually her life turned inwards. By the time her illness was diagnosed there was no-one to support her. She was suspicious of strangers and refused all welfare assistance except the community bus to Tesco once a week. She pretended she had a whole army of carers, close friends and family, but in truth there was no-one except an elderly man from a few doors down, Bernard Steadman, who called in three or four times a week on his way to the shops. She was glad of the chance to pass the time of day and he was occasionally useful, but he was not someone she could rely on.

'Morning, Helen, how are you today?'

'Don't ask. My back's been playing up all night.'

'Can't the doctor give you anything for it?'

'No, I've got all these painkillers and anti-inflammatories but they don't do any good.'

'Do you want anything from the Co-op?'

'You could get me some money from the machine. £100 should be enough.' She really needed some more cigarettes and another bottle of wine, and the whisky was getting low, but couldn't ask Mr Goody-two-shoes, as Colm called him. Nor could she wait for her visit to Tesco. She'd have to wait for Colm to come back. He was always so obliging.

She hobbled back to the kitchen, nearly tripping down the step. Now in her seventies, Helen was struggling. The house was beyond her, four floors of rotting Victorian semi-detached just off the Hove seafront. The building next door had been rented to the council who used it as a temporary hostel. She should have moved years ago: now it was too late. It would have to see her out.

'Could you not convert it into flats, Mrs Betteridge?' It seemed Colm had some experience of property development. 'I know someone who could have a look at it for you.'

'And where would I get the money?'

She had a bit put by, but that was mainly for emergencies. In the winter she could barely afford the heating bills. With her thin frame and slow movements, she was often cold and wrapped in layers of woolly cardigans and Viyella vests. In the summer, as now, she wore flimsy but voluminous dresses which flowed around her bare legs, white and veined like Danish blue, her feet stuffed in old sandals. She didn't care for herself as before. Her wispy hair fell around her face; make-up was a thing of the past. She used to be very fussy about the way she looked, always pausing before the full-length mirror on the turn of the staircase, examining her features, patting her hair in place, pulling in her tummy, but being disabled it was more difficult to keep herself looking good, and living alone it wasn't necessary. She no longer saw the mirror on the staircase for now she had to live on the ground floor. It was too much of a struggle to be going up and down stairs every day.

Colm didn't seem to mind. He lived on the first floor. The two highest floors were empty. He was supposed to have just the one bedroom and bathroom, and share the downstairs kitchen, but he'd sort of spread out.

'You don't mind if I store some of my stuff, do you? Tell you what, I'll clear those other bedrooms for you if you like, tidy them up. They need a bit of an airing.' He paused and peered into her eyes. 'You know there's a lot of work needs doing upstairs. I've been looking. Some of the woodwork's rotten, and there's a lot of damp on those back walls. You've never thought of selling this place, have you? You could buy yourself a nice little flat on the seafront. Make yourself comfortable.'

'No, Colm. I can't be moving at my age. I'll never move now.'

'Are you sure there? I know someone who could be interested.'

'I said No, Colm.'

'Ok, I'll say no more, but you think about it. Anyway, you don't mind me storing some stuff, do you?'

There had been a steady stream of cardboard cartons of all shapes and sizes coming and going ever since. He had a trailer hitched to his car. Helen didn't know where the trailer came from, but it wasn't long before it became part of the landscape.

‘I thought next weekend if it’s fine I’d have a go at clearing the drive and back garden.’ It was all overgrown and full of rubbish. ‘Then I can park in the drive – you wouldn’t mind?’ he’d added.

The next weekend was scorching. Colm had hired a skip and got a couple of friends along to help. Helen was a bit surprised by the friends. Colm was a smart young man, soberly dressed, neat short hair, sensible shoes, but his friends, a man and a girl, both Irish, seemed rough and coarse, especially the girl who had huge gold earrings, unkempt ginger hair, and wore torn jeans and just a suntop, none too clean. She had a runny nose and kept wiping it with the back of her hand. They hadn’t come into the house, not once, and looking out the back she’d seen them drinking beer straight from the cans. What they’d done when they’d needed the toilet she didn’t want to know.

‘Would you all like a cup of tea?’ she’d asked Colm.

‘No, thank you, Mrs Betteridge, don’t you worry.’ He gave a dismissive wave.

After the friends had gone, he asked, ‘You wouldn’t mind if I park the trailer round the back, would you, Mrs Betteridge.’

She tried to refuse, but the alternative was to have the trailer parked in the drive at the front. Besides was easier for him to carry his stuff in through the back door, she could see that. There had been so many boxes, something to do with work, but she couldn’t remember what.

He regularly parked his car in the driveway. It was his one ostentation, an old but immaculate bright red BMW convertible. She thought it gave the house a bit of tone. And the cats loved sitting on the folding roof, though they left their muddy pawprints all over the bonnet. They were the only things she cared for; they were so playful, so full of fun. She called them Laurel and Hardy.

Colm and Helen sat together in the sun just outside the back door. Colm had brought out two kitchen chairs and a small table, two glasses, a bottle of red and the bottle of whisky, and the ashtray. He poured Helen a glass of red.

'Time enough for the good stuff later.'

She lit a cigarette, patted her lap for Laurel to jump up, and took a long draught of wine.

'You spoil me, you do.' She chuckled.

'Well now, you've been very good to me, Mrs. Betteridge, and I had something else to ask you about.'

'What's that, dear?' She was feeling very mellow.

'It's my cousin, it is. Him and his friend they're over from Ireland and don't have anywhere to stay. I thought they could stay here till they find somewhere to live.'

'I don't know, Colm. Where would they sleep?'

'There's a couple of old beds on the top floor. I thought I could clear some of my boxes and put up the beds in the back bedroom.'

'When have you been up to the top floor? That should be all closed off.'

'That's what I thought, but it isn't. I heard noises up there the other day when you were out at Tesco, so I had a look around. I think it might have been the cats. Anyway, all the doors are closed now. What do you think? You don't mind, do you? It won't be for long. My cousin's a builder, that he is. We could ask him to fix the roof around that back chimney stack; there's a lot of damp got in on those upper floors.'

'I don't know about that. I can't be paying for building work.'

'No, I know that. But my cousin could do it for nothing.'

'Well, all right then, but just you just make sure they behave themselves. They can't stay for long.'

'That's wonderful, Mrs Betteridge. I'll text them. I

should think they could be here tomorrow. Here, let me pour you a glass of the hard stuff.'

'You're spoiling me wicked, you are.'

When they arrived, there were two men and a girl.

'Oh, did I not mention, Mrs Betteridge, my cousin had another friend who might be with them?'

More alarmingly, she thought she recognised the girl.

'Is that the girl who helped with clearing the garden?'

'You mean, Caitlin? No, this is her first time over here. Now you mention it, I can see there's a resemblance, but no, it's not her.'

They towered over Helen in the hallway about to go upstairs, lugging a variety of plastic sacks.

'So, this is Caitlin, Mrs Betteridge.' An awkward silence followed.

Caitlin sniffed. 'Pleased to meet you,' she said.

'And this is Connor.'

Connor nodded.

'And this is Dylan.'

Dylan looked at the floor.

Then they all went up the stairs. Colm led the way, telling them where to go, leaving Helen alone by the kitchen door watching them. Her head had started to feel fuzzy. It was like watching a movie in which she didn't have a part. She could hear them tramping through the rooms, floorboards creaking. Then they all came down again and went outside. Through the frosted glass of the front door, she saw Colm's bright red car being moved out of the driveway, then a much bigger vehicle going in. There was barely room. She heard Colm.

'Left a bit, back, back, whoah. Back a bit more.'

She hobbled down the step through to the kitchen side window to see better. They had an old bus, and there were curtains and old blankets across the windows. They must have been sleeping in it. She had never encountered people like this before. She didn't know what to say to them, how they might react. They were surly and unkempt, nothing like Colm. He was smart and neat and polite. How could these people be his cousins and friends? And if they weren't, then who on earth were they?

At first her worst worries were assuaged. There wasn't much noise from upstairs, and her new lodgers were out all day and often didn't return until late evening. But after a few days Helen saw a small truck parked in the drive. It was a dull khaki colour, no windows other than the windscreen, high wire mesh sides, and huge muddy tyres.

Connor and Dylan had got out and started bringing stuff in from the truck through the kitchen, old bits of carpet, blankets, pots and pans, a kettle, a microwave and an electric hob, two old televisions, and heaven knows how many black plastic sacks.

'Colm said it would be OK,' mumbled Connor, barely looking at her.

She complained to Colm as soon as he got in from work. 'It's so they don't disturb you, Mrs Betteridge. They can't be sharing the kitchen, can they? They need their own things.'

'But why have they brought in all this stuff, Colm? I thought they were only going to be here for a few days. They can't just move in, you know.'

'No, no, don't you worry your head about that, Mrs Betteridge. They'll be gone in no time and you'll never know they were here.'

'This is my home, Colm. I must remind you, you are the lodger. I've got my rights.' She pressed an index finger down on the worktop.

'Sure you have Mrs Betteridge, and I'm beholden to

you. You've been very obliging, I'm sure.' He had this habit of wringing his hands and hunching his shoulders, his face somewhere between a smile and a cringe. 'It won't be for long.'

'Well, just you make sure they don't outstay their welcome.'

He didn't seem to want to give any more assurances. Instead, he said, 'Now, can I be bringing you anything back when I'm out tomorrow.'

'No thank you, Colm. I expect Bernard will be going to the Co-op in the morning.'

Bernard was peering round the corner of the drive as he waited for her to come to the door.

'What's all this then, Helen?'

'They're friends of Colm. I'm not happy with him, not at all.'

'They look as if they're moving in.'

'Well, I hope not.' She stopped to cough. 'Colm says they're here just a few days until they've found somewhere to live.'

'It seems like they already have. Now, is there anything you want from the Co-op?'

Bernard got his instructions and trooped off. By the time he came back she was sitting in the kitchen looking worried.

'Are you all right?'

'I don't know, Bernard. I feel a bit funny. I went all dizzy.' Her voice sounded a bit slurred. He sat down and peered at her through his glasses. 'Helen, have you felt like this before?'

'Well, come to think of it I did have a bit of a turn a few days ago,' she said. 'It was after I'd had a drink with Colm in the garden. I thought it was the whisky.'

'I think you should go to the doctor. Who's your GP?'

‘I don’t like bothering with Doctors,’ she said, but she was leaning forwards with her elbows on the kitchen table staring at the plastic cloth and when she looked up at Bernard again, she said. ‘Perhaps I should, though. I’m thinking something’s not quite right.’

Bernard got an appointment for later that same morning.

‘Is there anything else I can do? How will you get there? Shall I arrange for a taxi?’

But not long afterwards it was Colm who took charge. He happened to be back early. When he learnt what had happened and about the GP appointment, he would have none of it.

‘They’ll have a look at you and then send you straight off to A&E,’ he said. ‘Take my advice and get yourself down to A&E straightaway. Cut out the middle-man, ay?’

‘But I can’t be getting a taxi all the way over there, Colm. Lord knows how much it would cost.’

‘Better than that, I’ll take you,’ said Colm, and she could see he meant it. ‘I’ll drive you there, wait, and bring you back again.’

She was secretly relieved that Colm had taken charge. Bernard was a bit of a weed, and Colm had the car and seemed very much in control.

A&E reception was a wooden cubby-hole set in a grey plastered wall covered in notices. Rows of metal stacking chairs were set in lines in front of it. But in less than five minutes Helen was being examined in a clean cubicle with white walls and blue curtains. The doctor, an eager little man with a beatific smile and a faint Geordie accent nodded as he spoke, as if in agreement with himself.

‘Mrs Betteridge, I think you’ve had what we call a transient stroke. You’re all right now, but I’d like you to have a few tests. Is there anyone waiting for you?’

'Yes,' she said. 'My lodger brought me in his car.' She closed her eyes. Her instinctive resistance abandoned her and she allowed herself to be looked after. A nurse was dispatched to find Colm. She was a sharp featured blond with a brisk and efficient manner. She led him down a long gleaming white corridor full of trolleys and other obstacles, speaking over her shoulder. Colm tried to keep up.

'We want her to have some tests, and to make sure she's stabilised. We don't want to discharge her until we're sure she can manage. Does she live on her own?'

'Yes, she looks after herself. I'm the lodger but I take care of her when I can. She's a bit unsteady on her feet she is.'

'We'll want her to be here overnight, then we'll see how things are tomorrow.'

Colm was ushered in behind the curtains.

'Now, Mrs Betteridge, don't you be worrying, you'll be alright, you will. Just tell me if there's anything you want me to bring.'

'But you won't know where anything is, Colm, and I don't want you going through my things. I don't want you in my rooms. They're private.' Her voice was rising in intensity.

'Don't worry, Mrs. Betteridge. I'm not going into your rooms if you don't want me to. Tell me, are there any relatives you'd be wanting to tell you're in the hospital. Is there anyone else who you'd like me to tell?'

'I don't have anyone; you know that Colm. You can tell Bernard, so he knows not to call in. He lives at no.16, that's three doors down, basement flat, and if I'm not back later today, you can feed the cats.'

'Course I will. Now is there anything else I can help you with?'

'If you want to help you can tell that Connor and his friends to get out of my house.'

'Now then, Mrs Betteridge, don't you be worrying about them. They won't be going into your rooms, will they?'

'But when are they leaving? It's nearly three weeks since they moved in. I don't want them around if I'm away. You never know what might happen. I don't know what I was thinking of, letting them into the house.'

'Oh, but it will be fine. I'll be there to keep an eye on things. I'll make sure everything's looked after. You just get some rest an' all. The sooner you're better the sooner you'll be back.'

Two days later, Helen was sitting in the corridor beside the alcohol gel dispenser outside the ward. She had her stick and was wearing the same clothes she'd had on when she was admitted. She was waiting for Colm. He'd left his daytime contact details, but she'd been unable to manage the long sequence of numbers for his mobile and the staff nurse had dialled for her. Helen was armed with a pile of tablets, nicotine patches, and severe warnings against smoking and drinking alcohol.

'Well, they always give these warnings, do they not?' said Colm as he helped Helen into the car. 'Course you've got to be careful, but you can't be doing with giving up all your pleasures, can you now?'

He drove back along the seafront. The car was immaculate. So was his driving. They swung up the avenue towards the house.

'Here, let me take that for you,' he said, gesturing to the bag of prescriptions on the back seat. 'Now you just sit here while I go in and get the back door unlocked.'

He had parked halfway down the drive to be near the side entrance to the kitchen.

‘So, they’re still here I see,’ said Helen, waving her hand towards the old bus and ghastly khaki truck as Colm helped her into the house.

‘Just for now, Mrs Betteridge, just for now.’

He helped her inside and she plonked herself down by the kitchen table with a sigh. Colm was highly attentive.

‘You’ll be wanting a cup of tea, Mrs Betteridge. And later on, I’ll get you something to eat.’

She examined the kitchen. Everything looked as it had before. She thought she’d have a rest, get tidied up a bit, change her clothes.

‘That’s very kind, Colm. I’ll see you later,’ and she reached for her stick and hobbled towards the hallway. ‘Don’t help me: I’ve got to try and do this for myself.’

She was halfway along the hallway when she heard someone running down the stairs and found herself face to face with a complete stranger, a skinny girl, late teens or early twenties, wearing a skimpy dress, nothing else, barefoot, laughing.

‘Who the hell are you?’ Helen drew herself upright and stood leaning on her stick.

‘Who the hell are you, more like?’ The girl laughed in her face, pushed past her, and ran down the hall into the garden.

Before Helen could recover, she heard Connor thudding down the staircase. He stopped when he saw Helen. Colm rushed out of the kitchen.

‘Connor, see who we have here. Mrs Betteridge is back from hospital. I’m looking after her. You’ll be on your way back upstairs. I’ll be up in a minute. I’ll just deal with Mina first.’

He turned to Helen. ‘I’m really sorry about that, Mrs Betteridge. She shouldn’t have said that. I’ll have a word with her, be sure it won’t happen again.’

‘But who is she, Colm?’

‘Mina: Mina’s her name. She’s a friend of Caitlin’s.’

‘I hope you’re not going to tell me she’s living here as well?’

‘I think she’ll just be visiting. Now if you’ll excuse me, I’ll go and teach her some manners, and you forget all about this and go and get some rest.’ He went out to the garden.

Helen was even more shocked by what happened next. Her bedroom window was open and she could see Colm and the girl reflected in the windscreen of the bus. Colm had grabbed the girl’s bare arm and was shaking her. She heard snatches of conversation.

‘I didn’t know who she was, did I?’

‘You stupid little slut. Who did yr’ fucking think it was?’

‘An’ we have to be nice to ’er? To that old slag?’

‘She owns the house, you boggin gippo.’

Helen didn’t hear anymore. Mina had kicked out at Colm, and he’d hit her in the face, her grabbing at him. Both of them fell onto the gravel behind the bus. Then Colm was back on his feet, again grasping Mina’s arm, her wiping her face with her free hand. He dragged her round the side of the house out of Helen’s sight and there were more thuds and wails. They came in through the back door, Mina snivelling, Colm hushing her as he bundled her up the stairs. Shortly afterwards there was muted cursing and raised voices back and forth, then footsteps quietly downstairs and past her bedroom. It sounded like Colm had come back down to the kitchen. She sat on the edge of her bed leaning forwards as she strained to hear if the footsteps were coming back again. She stared at the door handle, hunched up and willing it not to open.

She had never heard Colm swear, never an impolite word, always courteous, never aggressive. Her head began to throb and she lay back on the pillows. She was asleep within seconds, her mouth hanging open, her breath rasping in her throat.

She'd thought about telephoning the police but agonised over the consequences. What would she tell them? What if they couldn't do anything? What if Colm left with the others? How might he react? Who would take care of her afterwards? She couldn't manage on her own. Her world had reduced to the short walk between the kitchen, her bathroom and her bedroom. She was having difficulty with her balance and was getting double vision. Watching the television strained her eyes. She couldn't even bend down to feed the cats, and Colm had to see to them in the mornings. For much of the day she sat in her room listening to the radio or dozing. She didn't like being in the kitchen anymore. People would come in from the back door into the hallway at any time of the day or night.

Her weekly trip to Tesco on the Community Care bus was a thing of the past. Colm volunteered to order the supermarket shop online and get it delivered: 'You shop and we drop,' as it said on the van. Of course, Colm had had to have her bank details to set up the Tesco account, but she'd already given him her pin-number so he could get her cash from the Co-op machine rather than having to ask Bernard. He'd proved entirely trustworthy, always keeping receipts and being punctilious about counting the notes in front of her.

She'd been used to Bernard with his visits to the Co-op, but there was nothing for Bernard to get for her because Colm had got it all already. Then one morning she was in the front room when Bernard rang the doorbell and Colm opened the door almost immediately; he must have been standing in the hall. She heard Bernard's usual greeting.

'How are you, Colm, and how's Mrs Betteridge today?'

'I'm grand thanks, and Mrs B, she's a fine lady now, isn't she? She's resting at the moment, but I'll tell her you called.'

'I wondered if there's anything she'd like from the Co-op?'

'No, there's no need, Bernard. I'm able to get her shopping. I can save you the trouble.'

'It's no trouble, I'm sure.'

'She's often resting now in the mornings. It's best not to disturb her.'

From behind the curtains, Helen watched him go, like a lifebelt slowly drifting beyond her reach. Not much of a lifebelt, she thought, more like a bit of old frayed rope. He wasn't the sort to interfere.

But it was with alarm that she discovered Colm was no longer protecting her as well as he had at the beginning. He seemed to allow anyone into the house. When she got up in the mornings to go down the hall to her bathroom, she had no idea whom she might meet. People just came and went as they pleased. She started to worry about her belongings and rummaged in the kitchen drawer to find the keys to her living room and bedroom. More than once, she had gone to her bathroom to find the toilet seat up and the pan yellow with urine. Colm had to fix a bolt on the inside of the door because she was terrified of someone coming in when she was on the loo or getting washed. Then there was the noise. It wasn't just people going up and down the stairs and in and out of the house, but raised voices, swearing, music of all sorts from heavy thumping rock to fiddles and mouth organs. Helen half hoped the neighbours would complain but feared the trouble it would cause.

The other occupants of her house, "my house", as she reminded Colm, behaved like animals. Every so often someone would bring a stinking black bag downstairs, heavy with sodden waste, and chuck it in the garden. Foxes and seagulls tore it apart. And there were fights, she knew. She could hear the crashes and curses from above, and not just the men; the women, only girls some of them, were just as bad. She was convinced that Mina was one of the worst.

Then one night the cats went missing. She felt certain they were in the house somewhere. She begged Colm to search the upper floors and reluctantly he went up and started opening doors. Suddenly she heard a yell and cursing, scrabbling noises, and both cats shot down the stairs and bolted into her bedroom. They cowered under the bed behind the valance and would not come out again. Colm appeared in the doorway.

'Jaysus, jaysus, what in God's name has got into those cats?'

She hardly heard him.

'What have you done?' she cried. 'What have you done to my babies?' She was down on her hands and knees reaching under the bed.

'I haven't done anything, Mrs. B. I went up there to find them for you, didn't I?' He knelt beside her on the floor. 'Come on, Mrs B. They won't come out now. Something's frightened them. Here, let me help you.'

He helped her upright and backed her towards the chair beside the bed. He had deep scratches on his arms, saliva and dirt and blood on his white shirt.

'Why, you're hurt?' she said.

'I'll be all right. You stay here, Mrs. B. I'll just go and find some plasters and be right back.'

He returned a few minutes later with a box of plasters, a cloth and a washing up bowl half-full of warm water and disinfectant. Also, a bottle of whisky and two glasses.

'I think we could both do with one of these,' he said. 'What a carry on.'

'They won't come out from under the bed. Where did you find them, Colm?'

'Ahh, one of those rooms on the top floor. I can't remember.'

'What, just in the room by themselves?'

'No, they'd got into a cupboard somehow. I opened the cupboard door and they were in the corner. They wouldn't come out. When I put my hand in to get them, they went crazy, spitting and clawing, bloody things.'

She could get no more out of him, and it took her ages before she could coax the cats out from under the bed. They'd pooed on the floor and cowered and growled whenever she went near them. They were forever licking themselves. They seemed to be covered with soot. It was days before she was able to examine them properly. There was visible bruising to the outside of Laurel's ears and both seemed to be missing bits of fur. Most disturbing, they had what seemed to be scorch marks on their tails and behinds.

'This is to get at me, isn't it, torturing my cats,' she told Colm. 'It was that girl, Mina. I'm going to phone the RSPCA.'

'You mustn't do that, Mrs Betteridge. We'll never get to find out how this happened. We don't want people like the RSPCA poking their noses in. You don't know what it'll lead to.'

'Whatever do you mean, Colm?'

'I mean the police. The RSPCA may call the police.'

'Well, what if they do? Perhaps I should phone the police.'

'For God's sake, Mrs Betteridge, for your own sake, don't do it.'

'Why not? I should have done it before. I'm not frightened of the police.'

‘Well, you should be, because you’re the one who could go to jail. Some of those scumbags upstairs are illegals, aren’t they? You’re giving them shelter. And what if the police find drugs, or stolen goods. You’re the one who’s keeping them, aren’t you? You’re the householder. Not me. I’m just the lodger.’

She was silent at this. She had never knowingly broken the law and was frightened by authority. Her mind sank into a muddle. Colm let the silence flow, like a river carrying flotsam into a deep pool.

‘Mrs Betteridge. You know I said I knew someone who might be interested in buying this house? I could perhaps see if he’s still of the same mind. It would be a good opportunity for you, wouldn’t it?’

‘I don’t know, Colm. Look at the state it’s in. I couldn’t sell it like this.’

‘Well, I think you’ll find it’s worth a lot, even in this condition. You’d have enough left over to buy yourself a nice new apartment.’

‘I’m not sure. I don’t know what to do. I’m too old to move.’

‘No, you’re not. I’d help you. You think about it, Mrs Betteridge, before it’s too late.’

The next day, as if on cue there were some new noises among the general hubbub, knocking and hammering and banging. At first Helen thought it was workmen in the road but then realised it was coming from inside the house. Colm didn’t seem to be around so she couldn’t ask him. Her alarm grew when she saw the khaki-coloured truck pull into the drive and two burly men in overalls carrying heavy tool bags into the house. They were followed by Caitlin and Mina with yet more black sacks. Halfway through the afternoon she was in her bedroom trying to rest when she heard a series of awful thuds which shook the house – far, far worse than anything previously. These continued, on and off, for the rest of the day, sometimes interspersed with jeers and yells. She waited all evening for Colm to come back, but in vain. He did this sometimes, just went off without warning for a day or two, then reappeared with no explanation.

The thudding and banging started again in the morning, accompanied now by the sounds of tearing timber and breaking glass. Clouds of dust were drifting down the stairs. Every so often the two big swarthy men in overalls would struggle down the stairs lugging huge canvas sacks of rubble and emptying them in the garden.

Helen struggled out of the kitchen to intercept them on their way back.

'Who are you? What are you doing?' she cried, but they looked at her blankly.

'What are you doing?' she cried again.

'Mi ne govori engleski.' They pushed past her up the stairs, and she stood at the foot of the banister looking up the stairwell to see them turn at the second-floor landing. After a few minutes the dreadful sounds of tearing timber and falling plaster began again. She went into her front room and put on the television. It helped drown out the noise, but she still could feel the vibrations. With shaking hands, she poured herself a whisky, sat down in her special chair and peered across the room through the net-curtained window to the street outside. Bernard stood on the pavement looking up at the house and peering at a big wooden sign in the driveway. Helen was suddenly desperate. He was her last and only hope. She tried to get to her feet, but too quickly; her head started to swim and, in her haste, she knocked over her stick. Precious seconds were lost. Whimpering with anxiety she limped across the room to pull aside the net curtains and wave, but she was too late. He was on his way already. Looking out of the bay window she could just make out the sign in the driveway. 'Abramovic & Lovric. Builders,' it said.

Helen spent the rest of the day in her bedroom. The cats were under her bed again; they hadn't eaten or gone out in days. They hadn't used their litter tray and had sprayed in the corners of the room. Once the banging had stopped and it seemed the men had gone, they emerged, all three, like refugees, to go to the kitchen. Her old sandals and their tiny paws left footprints in the dust in the hallway. She scraped some cat food into two bowls which she left on the worktop, found a sausage roll and a banana for herself, and they all padded back across the hall to hide in the bedroom.

She was woken by a soft knocking on the door.

'Mrs Betteridge, Mrs Betteridge, it's me, Colm. Open the door.'

It took a while, but eventually she crept out of bed, got her stick and felt her way to the door. Colm helped her back and sat beside her on the bed.

'This must be dreadful for you,' he said, 'all this mess.'

'I'm frightened.' She clutched at his arm. 'I don't know what's happening to me.' She started to cry.

'Don't you go upsetting yourself now. Have you thought any more about selling the house? You've got to think of yourself, haven't you, what's in your best interests an' all.'

'Oh Colm, you'll have to help me. I don't know what to do.'

'Sure, I'll help you, Mrs Betteridge. We'll sort it all out in the morning. You just get yourself some sleep.'

The builders left the following day. Colm seemed nervous, even more obsequious than usual. By the time Helen was up he had already phoned his contact.

'I was right. We're in luck. He's still interested. He'll pay up to £600,000. What with the condition of the house an' all he said it's not worth any more, but like I said, that'd be more than enough to buy yourself a lovely flat on the seafront. I'd like to help you if I may. It'd be no trouble to help a lady like you.'

Three months have gone by, it's October, and a strong south-westerly wind is blowing, kicking up little waves. Helen looks out of the living room window of her flat. The glazed balcony overlooks the seafront by the old West Pier. There's a smart wood panelled lift and she can get out into Regency Square and round the corner to the local shops. Each time she goes out she stops by the full-length mirror in the foyer, pats down her hair, pulls in her tummy. She can get about with a zimmer frame, and even uses the Age Concern bus to go to the supermarket. She goes on outings twice a week. Last week she went to Nyman's Gardens.

Her flat is plenty big enough for one, the cats are getting used to it, and there was more than enough money left over after the moving costs were paid. Colm had been a great help finding the flat and helping her move. Whatever would she have done without him? He called round from time to time to see how she was settling in. They usually had a glass of wine together on the balcony.

It had been an investment company, Irish, from Skibbereen she'd noticed on the contract, McCarthy Regeneration Ltd. which had bought her big old house.

'That's your name isn't it, Colm McCarthy?' she'd asked.

'Sure it is, Mrs Betteridge. But it's not me that's buying your house now, is it? I told you I knew someone: they're all McCarthys in Skibbereen.'

That same evening Colm was sitting in the kitchen of her

old house. It was the only habitable room; the whole building was being gutted and refurbished. There would be eight "luxury" apartments at £350,000 each. His private army were presently encamped along the seafront by the King Alfred Leisure Centre, maybe heading for Eastbourne. Colm had the "personal" ads. pages of the Eastbourne Herald spread out in front of him.

"Peaceful little room on first floor of house off
Eastbourne Esplanade.
Access to kitchen and bathroom. Owner retired.
Would suit young professional man or woman.
£300 per week. Rent includes –
water, gas, electricity, wifi, council tax, tv, landline"

Colm picked up the phone. A woman answered.

'I'm phoning about the room,' he said. 'Is it still available? Perhaps I can come and see it?'

MATEUS ROSÉ

Emily has been waiting for him to come for well over an hour now. She's taken the day off work. Everything's ready. The fire is lit, the table is laid, two wine glasses arranged on the little table by the window together with a candle and a box of matches. She'd gone out earlier, especially to buy the wine glasses. She's loaded the record player with 6 EPs, spending half an hour choosing which ones to play, nothing too loud: Elvis's *Love me Tender*, followed by *Starry Eyed* and *Catch a Falling Star* by Michael Holliday, and then something far out, *Milord*, by Edith Piaf, for later.

Music was one thing, wine was another. She knows nothing about it and has to pore over the shelves in the off-licence. The labels mean nothing to her, the prices beyond her pocket, but what if she chooses the wrong type to go with the meal, the wrong vintage – is that even the right expression? Finally, she plucks up the courage to ask the assistant. He's not much older than her, fresh faced, cheerful, shoulder-length hair. She goes to the counter to get his attention.

'Er, I'm going to cook roast pork. It's a special occasion. Do you know what sort of wine I should have?'

Before he can reply she adds, 'It mustn't cost more than ten shillings.'

'I'd try this.' He hands down a bottle from a stack by the wall. 'Just in. Mateus Rose. Very romantic. OK?'

'Yes, thanks. Oh, do you have a cheap corkscrew, by any chance?'

She's cleaned the flat. She's brushed the dismal patterned carpet in the living room – purple cabbages, her Mother had called it – and hidden the awful Formica top of the dining table under a cloth. The sofa is camouflaged by a blue check rug with tassels on the sides. There's a small back-and-white TV with an indoor aerial beside the record player and an ugly tangle of wires in the corner hidden under the carpet. She hasn't been able to do much with the bedroom, but there are clean sheets on the bed and a fluffy orange rug on the linoleum beside it. She's hidden all her clutter in one of the drawers.

It's over four months since she met Fletcher, the first man she's really fancied since moving to London. She is dizzy with the thought of him. He's tall and well built, with a relaxed easy manner, and calls her "kid".

'How you doing, kid?' She savours the words on her tongue.

She couldn't believe her fortune when he'd first invited her out, and his obvious interest in her. But it's a fragile thing, interest. He's only been to the flat once when he helped her carry a set of bookshelves home and stayed for a cup of coffee. Thank goodness she'd got in some Maxwell House. The invitation to dinner was crossing a new threshold.

Fletcher was a Promotions Assistant with the Fruit Marketing Board in Dover Street. She used to work there as a temp on the switchboard. They'd met when he'd answered the phones for a day as part of his induction training. He was learning all about advertising and merchandising, consumer research, product development.

'It's exciting, isn't it?' she'd said. 'What you're doing, I mean.'

'It's the future,' he'd said. 'It's the way business is going.'

She'd taught him how to use the switchboard and listened to him talking to customers. He was very confident.

'Can I help?' he would say if a caller was unsure which department he wanted. 'No trouble, I'm sure,' she heard him say at the end of a call. Once he even said, 'No sweat.'

When he'd learnt she was only temporary and would be leaving shortly for a permanent job he'd asked if they could stay in touch.

'Where will you be working?'

'At the Ministry of Transport in Northumberland Avenue.'

'Not far away then. Perhaps we could meet up one lunchtime?'

A warm redness had crept up her neck and burnt her ears.

'I've only just got to know you,' he'd said. 'I can't let you disappear again.'

This is why she'd come to London, to find a new life, a new beginning. It had seemed such an exciting thing to do but there's been nearly six months of nights in front of the television, eating alone, sleeping alone. Living in an upstairs flat in Streatham Common she'd found it difficult to meet people.

She's taken pains with her hair. It's better down. Originally, she'd had the idea of putting it up, imagining him undoing the grips and pulling it down, stroking it like they do in the movies, but then he might not do that, and she looks better with it down. She's wearing a short sleeved red blouse. She'd worried this was too daring but it has a high neck and she wants something that buttons at the front, not a jumper. The blouse has cost her good money. It is nylon, "the new silk", and shiny and shows off the curves beneath. She has one good bra which is underwired which she hardly every wears, but she's wearing it now. Her skirt is tight at the waist and short above the knee. She's practised crossing her legs on the sofa in front of the mirror.

It's the first time she has cooked anything from a recipe. The cookery book, *Main Meals Cookery*, 2/-6d. lies open on top of the drawer unit in the kitchen. "Pork belly with Apple Sauce and Stuffing" is one of the recipes in the section "For entertaining".

She started cooking ninety minutes ago, but now she's had to turn it all off. The vegetables are cooked through. The pork joint lies on its side in the pan, grease beginning to congeal around it. Only the apple sauce is OK. It could be easily reheated, but what is the point?

For at least the twentieth time she looks at the clock. That's it, she was going to give him until 8.30, no longer, and now it's 9.00. If he's been held up or unable to come, why hasn't he phoned? There's the payphone in the hallway downstairs; he has the number. She picks up the pan and scrapes the pork into the bin, then chucks the vegetables and the apple sauce in after it. She pours the gravy down the sink, the mottled brown juices mixing with globules of fat as it slithers down the drain. She does all this roughly, the pans crashing and banging. She kicks the cupboard doors closed, scrapes the cutlery off the table and throws it into the drawer, all the while shaking her head, her eyes pricking with tears. The bottle of wine and the two glasses are still standing on the table. Emily fingers a glass. She could put her hands around it, she thinks, and squeeze and squeeze until it shatters, the shards slicing into the flesh of her palms and fingers. She puts it down again and takes up the corkscrew, twists it through the lead foil into the cork and pulls. At first nothing happens, then as she pulls harder the cork starts to split. Weeping, she tears the screw upwards and rams it back in again and again, bits of cork crumbling around the bottle neck, wine starting to leak past the corkscrew and dribbling onto the carpet, splashing over the chair.

Finally, she manages to force the cork down into the bottle. Sitting at the table and trembling, she pours herself a large glass, ignoring the bits of cork bobbing about, her hands shaking. She takes a gulp, and another. Her head begins to swim but so what? She drinks most of the bottle before suddenly feeling sick and running towards the bathroom, gagging, bile spilling from her mouth, then kneeling over the toilet, mouth open. There is sweat on her forehead and she is white and cold. She pulls herself half upright, puts the toilet seat down and sits on it, bent forward, head in her hands. After waiting for a few minutes, she feels strong enough to get up and walk back unsteadily to the lounge, still feeling a little dizzy, but the hurt has gone. She retrieves a bread roll out of the bin and flops onto the sofa.

When she wakes there's an old black and white movie about the second world war on the television. The wine bottle lies on its side on the floor, a rose-coloured stain spreading over the carpet. Cold and sour she gets to her feet, turns the TV off and stumbles to the bedroom, avoiding the mess on the floor, leaning on the furniture and walls for support. Sitting on the bed feeling heavy and faint it seems to take a peculiarly long time to unfasten her blouse and then it becomes stuck around her shoulders as she tries to take it off. She's sweating profusely. She wriggles an arm free. The skirt is easier and she rolls back on the bed and pulls the bedclothes over her, lying back on the pillows feeling her heart thumping, sweat running down her scalp under her hair and soaking the pillow. Her breathing is shallow and uneven.

When the alarm first goes off, she doesn't know what's happened. Cold reality arrives. What a little fool she is. She has to keep her eyes open if only to stop the recriminations inside her head. At first, she is barely able to walk. The state of the flat is beyond belief. She can't even begin to clear it up if she's going to get to work on time. For a moment she thinks about phoning the office and saying she is ill, but she can't. It's a matter of pride. Her head is throbbing, but she splashes her face, drinks a large tumbler of water and swallows two aspirin. She will concentrate her energies on having a wash and getting herself ready and to work on time. The flat can wait. She'll clear it up this evening.

The bus is late, it's pouring with rain, and her journey to Trafalgar Square takes longer than it should. She is late for work for the first time ever. She creeps in the side entrance reserved for the lower grade staff and gets her timecard stamped in the machine, the first black mark on her record: 09.15, Friday, March 1st.1968. She walks as fast as she can (running is not allowed) along the dark brown corridor which leads to central services and, in a purpose-built annex off the mail room, the main switchboard. She hangs up her coat behind the door and upends her umbrella in the metal waste-paper bin before sitting down on her swivel chair and picking up the headphones. Her head is spinning.

'Christ, you look terrible.' Cheryl is a fat happy girl with giant gold hoops for earrings, big bright red lips and a beehive haircut. Her super-short skirt reveals a thigh greater in circumference than Emily's waist. Her bum overlaps her swivel chair like a pair of panniers.

'You ill or something?'

'I didn't sleep well,'

'I'd have stayed in bed if I was you,'

I bet you would, thinks Emily.

She struggles through the day. She is suddenly hungry at lunchtime and goes down to the canteen in the basement. Joining the queue in the corridor with its green paint, huge radiators and an uneven parquet floor sticky with dirt, she considers making a dash to Dover Street to see Fletcher face-to-face but doesn't want to make an exhibition of herself. She doesn't even know if he's there and can't afford to be back late. She'll phone him instead. She gets herself a ham and cheese sandwich, the dry white bread curling at the edges, and takes it back upstairs so that Cheryl can go off for her lunchbreak. Emily needs to be on her own. Private phone calls are strictly forbidden without managerial approval and usually only granted in the event of extreme emergency. So what! She decides to phone Fletcher and demand an apology. She's surprised by her boldness, but her anger has been boiling up inside all day. She phones the Fruit Marketing Board.

'Putting you through now.' There is a long wait while the phone rings and rings. Eventually a man, not Fletcher, picks it up.

'Three-four-eight-six.'

'May I speak to Fletcher, please?'

'He's away today. Can I help?'

'No, thanks. It was Fletcher I needed to speak to.'

'He might be back before knocking off for the day. Would you like to ring again? May I tell him who called?'

'No, thanks. It's OK.'

Why didn't he turn up last night? If he couldn't come,

why hadn't he let her know? Why hasn't she heard from him? Why didn't he ring? Her mood darkens. She wants to hit out at something, to shout at him, only he isn't there to be hit. And something keeps tugging at her train of thought, Fletcher's voice when they set the date. 'How could I forget?' he'd said. Well, he'd bloody well had, hadn't he? She gets through the rest of the afternoon, snapping at callers, yanking out the connections, dialling furiously.

'I've never seen you like this,' says Cheryl. 'What's happened? Can I help?'

'No! You can't,' says Emily, frowning and biting her lip until it hurts in an effort to stay in control, struggling to maintain her natural politeness. 'Just leave it, OK?' They fall silent. 'Thanks though,' she adds. 'I'll be alright.'

She'll go home, sort out the flat, have an early night. Try to forget. She walks out into Northumberland Avenue and back into the drizzle to join a huge queue at the bus stop. Arriving home later than planned she knows she must tackle the flat. She changes, putting on an old jersey and a brown knee length skirt which she uses only for housework. It takes her the best part of an hour to clear the mess in the kitchen and she turns her attention to the broken glass and the wine stains in the living room. Even worse are the stains left behind in her rush to the toilet. She scrubs at the carpet on her hands and knees with a grim determination, each brushstroke helping to erase the memories of the last 24 hours and with a cringe of shame she looks at the clock on the mantelpiece, 7.30pm. Yes, it is precisely 24 hours ago that this nightmare began.

The doorbell rings. She isn't expecting anyone. She looks a mess. There's no way anyone is going to be let into the flat. Perhaps if she doesn't answer whoever it is will go away. But she trembles with apprehension. It rings again, longer this time. Oh God, she thinks, it can't be! She pauses at the turn of the stairs. She can see the entrance porch down below through the landing window.

Fletcher stands on the step, his face bright and expectant, dressed in a smart suit with a narrow dark red tie and shiny pointed shoes. She draws back into the shadows, her mind replaying the last time she'd seen him.

He'd mentioned a conference in Brighton but that he should be able to get back in time. She remains hidden by the darkness on the stairs but peeps out again. Fletcher is carrying a large bouquet of daffodils and Michaelmas Daisies. Spring flowers, she thinks; he'd said something about spring when they were fixing the date.

He looks up, searching the first-floor windows, seeming quite sure of himself. Does he sense an observer in the shadows beyond the landing window? She holds her breath, immobile, her mind darting back once more to what Fletcher had said. Something about March 1st being the first day of spring, he'd made a sort of joke about lambs and rabbits and eggs. And all along she'd had it in her head that Thursday, yesterday, was March 1st. But the clock at work had said today was March 1st. She had sensed that something was wrong but had been distracted about being late for work. Now her whole body burns with embarrassment. She'd forgotten it's a leap year: yesterday was February 29th. The first day of Spring is today; the dinner date is this evening.

What a fool she has been! The bell rings again, echoing in the shared hallway downstairs. If she doesn't answer, the old man in the ground floor flat will probably go and answer it. From the shadows she can see Fletcher stepping back to get a better view of the front of the house. Too late she remembers she's left the lights on upstairs.

She feels her whole future hangs in the balance. She can't hide and pretend to be out. She can't admit her mistake.

Perhaps she can blame Fletcher and brazen it out. Her leaden legs carry her down the stairs. She opens the door.

Fletcher holds out the daffodils and Michaelmas daisies, half bowing, his words rehearsed: 'A bouquet for the first day of Spring.'

His expression changes as he sees her face, her old jersey, the brown skirt, the yellow rubber gloves.

His face breaks into a smile. 'It was tonight, wasn't it?'

Original title, **Main Meals Cookery,** Long Listed in West Sussex National 2016

FOR RICHER FOR POORER

What would you do with a million pounds if it just dropped onto the doormat? Pick it up? You bet you would. And what would you do then? Call out to the wife and kids – 'Hey guys, here's a million pounds on the doormat.'

Or would you keep it to yourself?

Other than the cream manilla envelope lying on the doormat it was a day like any other. Getting out of the house was always an obstacle race between four competing players – Peter, Susan and the two kids – but this morning he'd made it to the bathroom door first, found a suit which didn't need pressing, and persuaded Susan to make breakfast for Damien and Katy. By 8:45 he was already reversing the Volvo into the road and stood a good chance of being on time for work. He had paused only to check the post on the doormat, chucking the items addressed to him into the car.

He had a thing about the post, some deep need to know what was coming before anyone else, a mixture of worry over bills and bank statements, fear of what might pop up from the past, or what might lie round the corner – a medical check-up, a note from the school. Today there were a couple of bills and a cream manilla envelope, postmarked Hexham. He swivelled it around on the passenger seat when he stopped at the junction. On the front, Peter W Goldsmith, esq.. Very formal. On the back, in small type he squinted to read: 'Trubeck, Alderson, and Lowson: Solicitors.' He'd never heard of them.

The BMW behind hooted angrily; the lights had changed. He shoved his hand out of the window, middle finger thrust upwards. At the next lights he had to look away and pretend not to notice as the BMW pulled alongside. Suddenly he felt small and insecure, a bit pathetic. In the carpark he dragged a comb through his greying hair and re-adjusted his tie in the mirror. His face was drawn. He felt tired already, with the day hardly begun. But at least he was on time as he crossed the yard under the "Yorkshire Woollens" archway, pushed through the revolving door and took the lift to the accounts office.

It was mid-morning before he was alone. He slit open the cream manilla envelope with some trepidation. His Grandmother had died, aged ninety-six, in a nursing home in Barnard Castle. The solicitors acting for the estate wanted to meet him at their offices in Hexham. They recognised it was a lot to ask at short notice, but would he call Mr Trubeck to sort out dates? They needed Peter to read the will.

Peter was amazed. He had last seen his Grandmother over thirty years ago, he a teenager, his Grandmother very old even then, hobbling around on a stick, living alone, unloving and unloved in a rented cottage on the edge of the moor. It would be surprising if there was money enough for her funeral. Hermit-like, without a telephone and ignoring letters, she'd not even responded when her daughter, Peter's mother, had died. He phoned Trubeck as soon as he could be sure of being undisturbed. Trubeck would give no details over the phone but he confirmed there was a will and he, Peter, was the sole beneficiary. Peter arranged to go to Hexham the following Tuesday and yes, he'd be coming on his own.

Trubeck looked keenly at Peter. He cleared his throat self-consciously before saying, 'I suspect this may come as a shock. The estate is worth nearly two million pounds. After tax and costs, roughly £1.3 million.'

There was a short silence. Peter caught his breath, barely able to stop himself gasping.

'How?' There was a buzzing in his ears; he shook his head. 'How can it possibly be that much?'

Trubeck gave a rueful smile. 'Your grandad was a miser; whatever money he had he put into treasury bonds and gold mining shares. He was worth a fortune, but when he died your grandma had no interest in it, never touched it. Even in her nineties she still went to bed by candlelight and drew her water from the spring in the yard outside. The only reason she'd made a will, after some persuasion from me, was to prevent the government from getting their hands on it.'

Peter was hardly listening. His mind was full, wondering what to do. So far, no-one else knew. Susan didn't know about the letter, nor about his visit to Hexham. By a stroke of luck, he'd been due to attend an accounting course in Newcastle that week, and it had been easy to make a detour to Hexham on the way. He might be a bit late for registration, but he'd be there in time for lunch.

'I had absolutely no idea. My God. I don't know what to do.' He paused, then asked, almost in a whisper. 'Who else knows about this?'

Trubeck was aware of no-one, other than the bank and the tax man, who would learn about Peter's inheritance. The will would be a matter of public record of course, and the local paper might see a story in the old hermit leaving so large a sum, but with a bit of luck it would go no further.

Trubeck enquired, 'When do you want to tell the family?'

In a panic, Peter made his first fateful decision.

'Not yet,' he said. 'For the time being I would like to keep this to myself.'

And in the quiet of the hotel room later that day, Peter's mind was as busy as a disturbed wasp's nest. It was so tempting, so very tempting to go straight home, tell Susan the wonderful news, not bother with the accounting course, not even bother with going back to the office. In spite of himself he sought the support of the minibar, opened a miniature of whisky, and lay down on the bed. He needed to think this through. He began to realise that his good fortune had the potential to threaten the status quo, both at home and at work.

In many ways his present life was tolerable, not wonderful but comfortable enough. Work was a bit mundane and undemanding but he was a good accountant, easily on top of his subject and respected in the office. He felt secure in his present position. He was comfortable working in an environment where numbers had to balance and invoices and payments had to match. This was not quite the image Susan had of his work. Susan imagined something more managerial, but then Susan had a touching faith and no real knowledge of what he did, nor much interest in it. Peter had always kept a very firm separation between home and work. The office was a good forty minutes' drive away on the other side of Bradford. They never saw his colleagues socially. He lay back on the pillows, whisky in hand, and phoned Susan. He tried to sound normal.

'Hello, darling, how are you?'

'I'm fine. I was hoping you'd phone. I was going to phone you; I was a bit worried.'

'What's wrong? Is everything OK?'

'There's nothing wrong, it's only that someone from the course rang earlier to see if you were on your way.'

Peter's heart jumped. 'When was that, what did you say?'

'It was about one o'clock. I'd just got in from work. They wanted to be sure you were coming, that you hadn't cancelled or anything. I said you'd left here at about 9.00. I thought maybe you'd gone into work first.'

'Er, yes, I did,' said Peter. 'There was something I had to finish off.'

The explanation seemed credible; Susan had even suggested it herself. 'So, everything's all right then?'

'Yes, fine. What are you doing? Is the hotel OK?'

'It's nice enough. I'm just getting ready to go down to dinner.'

'Don't drink too much.'

Why did she always have to say that?

'Don't worry. I won't.'

Family life for Peter was comfortable. Did he have a happy marriage? He certainly defined himself by his family. They were the only family he'd ever been fully part of. He didn't quite understand why Susan seemed to look up to him so much but he was needy of her approval. They never had quite enough money, but they never really went without. Susan had a shared interest with another parent from the school in a flower shop and worked there part-time, the children were doing OK in school, they had a modest house in Harrogate, a large mortgage, two cars (Susan had an old Mazda roadster), holidays in French camp sites, ate out every couple of weeks. Their life together was familiar and uncomplicated, but Peter was constantly on guard against external threats, darting hither and thither like an insect protecting its nest, always fearful of the unexpected, the accidental.

And in a funny sort of way, a million pounds was a bit like an accident. It was enough to make a profound difference. It was not so much the thought of a bigger house or new car that exercised his mind, rather the realisation it would open opportunities previously never considered. With a million pounds he could buy himself into a partnership with a small firm of accountants or take a year's sabbatical to study for an MBA. Did he really want a career change when he was already happy enough in his present job? And what about Susan? Susan had long hankered after opening a bigger shop selling not just flowers, but also garden ornaments and maybe greetings cards and candles. Peter reckoned he knew Susan well enough to be wary of her business ability and he was enough of an accountant to know that a million pounds wouldn't go very far. If the news got out, he wouldn't be able to prevent an avalanche of expenditure from Susan and the kids.

On the other hand, a million pounds – in the bank – would provide a security blanket big enough to wrap around you for a lifetime, and if sensibly invested, would provide a nice supplementary income. He could use the interest to pay for all the little "extras" – evenings out, weekend breaks, better holidays, new clothes, maybe a better car for Susan, and still keep the security of the principal capital. If he was careful, he could disguise the additional income as salary increases, the reward for hard work and bigger responsibilities. Susan would be impressed. And their lives would be better, more comfortable, and hugely more secure, but – crucially – otherwise unchanged. This would all depend on keeping quiet, at least for now, and that might not be so easy. He'd already nearly been caught out going to Hexham. The first thing was to try and act normally. He would complete the accounts course in Newcastle as arranged and return home as if nothing out of the ordinary had happened.

But the weight of the secret became apparent even within a few minutes of arriving home. He was sitting down with Susan over a cup of coffee chatting about the course, the hotel, his journeys, when she said, 'Did it matter you were late arriving?'

'No, no; those first sessions are always a waste of time, just registration and introductions.'

Was it an innocent question or did she know he hadn't been to work first?

The conversation moved on, but Peter's discomfort wasn't over. Susan handed him the post. Amongst the bills and the junk there was a fat manilla envelope with the Hexham postmark.

'That arrived this morning,' she said, 'and that.' She pointed to an envelope from Lytham St Annes. 'I can tell it's from Premium Bonds. Maybe we've won a million.' Her mouth formed a little 'Ooh' in mock excitement.

Such was Peter's confusion that for a second he conflated the inheritance with the Premium Bond. Would opening one envelope reveal the secrets in the other? He handed back the premium bond envelope.

'You open it,' he said. His voice had become husky. 'Only £25.' Susan looked at him. 'Oh well, I suppose it's something. Maybe next time it'll be a million.'

The manilla envelope remained unopened on the table with the other mail. They both stared at it. Then, abruptly, Peter swept it up and went upstairs to unpack. All evening he waited for Susan to say something; she must have wondered why a firm of solicitors were writing to him, but the question remained suspended in the air.

Within a fortnight two more manilla envelopes from Trubeck had landed on the doormat to be scooped up into his bag and he'd been late for work three times, having to wait for the post to arrive before leaving home in the morning. This could not go on.

Three months later, he found himself pressing the entry phone of Sutcliffe Mailing Co. in Sheepcote Street, a grimy cul-de-sac at the back of Leeds Central Station. After several furtive visits and phone calls he had everything in place, a small company with an anonymous name – ABZ Investments – registered in the British Virgin Islands, and a UK company address at 32a Sheepcote Street, courtesy of Sutcliffe Mailing Ltd., with arrangements for all mail collection and receipt. Today he'd driven into Leeds during his lunch break to pick up his mail.

Ascending the stairs, he felt the stirring of a sense of ownership. However ridiculous, this dingy office contained the germ of something identifiably his. He revelled in the anonymity. The fat girl with the heavy mascara and jangly bracelets behind the desk in the upstairs office had no idea who he was, just a man in a raincoat come to collect his mail. In this small realm he was an actor on a different stage.

This stage extended to the internet. Like so many deceits, it had begun on a small scale. Sutcliffe Mailing automatically emailed Peter when mail was waiting for him. Peter was always careful to not to leave them in his in-box; his laptop was too readily available to the rest of the household. He knew the kids played games on it, in spite of dire threats if they were caught. But one day he'd come home to find Susan using his machine. There was nothing he could do. His eyes flew to the screen and back.

'What are you doing?' He tried to wash any anger or tension out of his voice.

'Oh, I can't get the internet on my laptop. I've been

trying all afternoon. I needed to look at my emails. Could you have a look at my stupid machine sometime? You don't mind me using yours in the meantime, do you?' She smiled. 'Or do you think I'm checking up on you?'

He didn't like what he saw behind her eyes.

'Only a joke,' she said.

Had she already looked at his inbox, maybe out of curiosity? He felt his face becoming red, heat rising across his chest and into his head.

'Hey, it's not a big deal,' she said. 'I won't be long; shall I leave it on when I've finished?'

'Yeah, OK.' He tried to sound offhand, but he knew his voice had fluttered. Had she noticed? Maybe not. Eventually she finished and went to get the dinner ready. Peter sat down in front of the machine. At first his hand was trembling too much to control the cursor. He opened his inbox and again his face flushed hot and red. There were three emails from Sutcliffe Mailing. It looked as if they'd been opened. He wasn't sure. They weren't necessarily incriminating, just lists of incoming mail, but nor were they easily explained. All evening he watched Susan's every movement to see if there were any questions hiding behind her eyes but learned nothing. He knew he couldn't risk this happening again.

He purchased a new laptop at a computer shop near his work and set it up one lunchtime before taking it home. He told Susan it belonged to work; he even wrote a stock number on it in black marker pen.

'These are only for senior staff,' he said. 'They're so I can work at home, or if I'm away on business. It gives me access to the HQ database, so I have to guard it like Fort Knox.' He searched Susan's face.

'I won't break into it, Guides honour. But seriously, they don't expect you to work at home, do they?'

'Well, it's better than having to stay late at the office.'

She looked a bit puzzled. 'But you never stay late.'

'Well, in case I have to,' he said, looking to see if that was a sufficient reply. She asked no more questions.

With his newfound freedom on the internet Peter trawled the financial and investment websites with his customary patience and attention to detail. He brought together a unique coincidence of business experience, numerical skill, complete privacy, and a shedload of money. The temptation was too great. For all his early determination to leave the million pounds dormant, he could not resist using some of it to speculate. In particular, he bought gold and oil. It was an inspired choice.

Early success bolstered his confidence. Eschewing an investment advisor, and anyway wanting to keep his privacy, Peter tested himself again and again against the market. Over the next four years he tripled his fortune. The fortune remained hidden, but like a surfer still impossibly upright on a wave growing ever higher. The more he speculated the more he was successful, and the more successful he was the more difficult it was to keep the secret. He was by now a seriously wealthy man.

So far, his luck had been almost too good to be true. His investments, however, were taking more and more of his attention, and far from enjoying his success he was coming under increasing strain from all sides. There was serious pressure on his time. Previously his day had been neatly divided, at work from nine until five, home in time for dinner. Now he had to find time, lots of it, to manage his growing fortune. He couldn't do much during working hours, but he'd always check the financial markets on arrival at the office, and every lunchtime he was on his mobile in the car park or huddled over his laptop in Starbucks or driving into Leeds to Sutcliffe Mailing. At home the pressure was even greater. Some evenings he would pretend to be doing office work. One weekday he'd had to make urgent conference calls and had left home at his usual time only to call in sick from his mobile phone and spend the whole day in a spare office at Sutcliffe Mailing. One Saturday he'd backed out of going to watch Leeds United with Damien. 'Sorry, mate, I've got all this work to do before next week.'

'You're always having to do work stuff. It's not fair.'

Often, he was caught between the thrill of the chase and the shame of cheating on family or colleagues. Did his colleagues think he was sloping off work and not pulling his weight? Was Susan worrying that he was becoming too stressed and working too hard?

It wasn't as if Susan couldn't see the benefits of all this hard work. Each of the last four years Peter had spun tales of salary increases and bonus payments. Susan still worked at the flower shop, but fewer hours, and the children had had some personal tuition and were doing well in school. They were able to participate in all those extra-curricular activities which had strained the family budget in the past – skiing holidays, swimming galas in Manchester, workshops at Opera North, geography field trips to the Lake District. Recent holidays had been in hotels rather than campsites, and in the Mediterranean rather than northern France. And Susan had a new Mazda roadster, in blue, and a whole new wardrobe of clothes. Peter was proud of these images of middle-class respectability, but there were other potential calls on the family finances which could not be satisfied without revealing the extent of his new found wealth.

Susan's parents had bought a tiny retirement cottage in Hornsea, "Lakeland by the Sea", fifteen years previously, but her dad had died within a year and her mum, Dorothy, had lived alone ever since. She was in her seventies and suffered from rheumatoid arthritis. Her doctor had said many times she should move away from the cold and damp East coast, but the price of Harrogate property was far beyond her. Susan had never even broached the subject with Peter; she knew the money wasn't there. The only reference was sometimes on a Saturday evening watching the National Lottery Draw and the inevitable daydream.

'If we won the lottery,' Susan would say, 'the first thing I'd do is buy Mum a little cottage nearer Harrogate, or perhaps do you think she'd like a little flat overlooking the Stray?'

Sat on his millions, Peter could go only along with the game.

'Perhaps in one of the villages,' he would reply. 'We wouldn't want her popping in all the time, now, would we?'

'Ooh, but it'd be lovely to be able to do something like that.'

'There's lots of things it would be lovely to do,' said Peter.

More affordable would have been Susan's idea to buy a bigger stake in the flower shop business. She had a half share, but there had been an opportunity to lease the small property next door and her partner had suggested they fund the expansion between them. Susan had lots of ideas for new products. She needed £12,000 and had asked Peter if he thought they could get a loan. She hadn't really thought he'd say yes but wasn't expecting to be dismissed out of hand.

'You must be joking,' he'd said. 'That business will never make any money. It's in the wrong position for a start. No-one's going to give you a loan to expand it. It'll be pouring good money after bad.'

She had tried to keep her temper. 'You've never supported it, have you. I suppose you think I should just stay at home and do the ironing. At least it's something I can do to bring in a bit of extra money. Don't forget who paid for our summer holiday last year!'

But there was no support from Peter, and the opportunity was lost.

Susan wasn't just disappointed; she was worried too. Peter had become increasingly pre-occupied of late, and he was irritable, and not just over money. It was difficult to put your finger on it, but he seemed less interested in the details of her day, or the children, more self-absorbed, too quick to claim that all was well and that he wasn't worrying about anything when he obviously was.

The other day Peter had arrived home early. Fleetingly Susan was pleased. 'Oh darling, you're early, this is nice.'

But he cut across her, face twisted, whether in remorse or irritation, she wasn't sure. 'No, I've got work to finish, it's hopeless at the office, I'm always being interrupted.' He tried to soften his tone. 'Look, I'm sorry. I need some peace and quiet. I'll be down in time for dinner.' He already had one foot on the staircase. He wouldn't look at her.

This time it was too much. 'Oh no, you're not going upstairs with that bloody computer again.'

Her voice broke. Susan didn't often complain, but the kids were out, she'd spent the afternoon on her own, and she'd been looking forward to Peter coming home. She needed reassurance, to spend time with him alone, to see his face when she spoke to him. But it was no good. Shoulders hunched, hurt like a small boy, he continued up the stairs. She shouted up after him.

'You're always hiding away. One of these days you're going to have to tell me what's wrong.'

More than ever, it seemed to Susan that there was a side to Peter that was hidden from her. Sometimes she wondered whether he was worried about money. Was that why he was working such long hours? Their finances seemed to be OK, but Susan had her doubts. There was the episode with the wallet. Peter had put it down on the dining table and she had moved it onto the sideboard as she was laying the table. As she did so, it came open and a small shower of credit cards fell out onto the floor.

'Damn,' she said. She was pressed for time. Katy had a dance class. She was bent down picking up the cards when Peter came into the room.

'I'll do it,' he almost shouted. 'You get on with the dinner.'

She frowned at the cards in her hand. In amongst the familiar NatWest and Nectar cards were a couple she'd never seen before, one from the Bank of Luxembourg and another from First Caribbean. He snatched them away.

'Are they new?' she said, still frowning.

'They're just trial offers,' he said. 'I'll never use them.'

Her eyes narrowed, but he thrust the cards back into the wallet and stomped out of the room.

Sometimes Susan wondered if there was another woman. Surely not. Surely she would know, although you heard such stories on the news, or TV dramas and suchlike. And there was that time a few months back when she mentioned her friend Sacha, who worked at an auditing firm in Leeds city centre.

'Sacha saw you near Leeds station at lunchtime,' she said. 'She hooted and waved but you weren't looking.'

Peter shrunk visibly, his shoulders hunched, his eyes cast sideways, but he was totally in denial.

'What does she mean? She must need her eyes tested. I hardly ever go into Leeds. I hope she doesn't spend all her lunchtimes hooting and waving at people. Of course it wasn't me. Lunch? Chance would be a fine thing. I don't have time for lunch.'

Susan dared not push him further.

He knew she wasn't totally convinced. The worst of it was, Peter could see what was happening: his whole life was becoming a lie. There was no-one to whom he could confide but he wanted to tell somebody. He'd become proud of his achievements. He fantasized of coming to the rescue of the family in some future crisis. Four years ago, he had been simply the lucky heir to an unexpected inheritance, but now he saw himself more as a successful investor, managing a fortune earned through his own skill and hard work. This was fast becoming the only part of his life which he felt good about, but for now it was still a hidden world, the grubby office around the back of Leeds station, the fat girl with the bangles at the reception desk, the private laptop.

It was around this time that another fateful envelope landed on the doormat at home – a buff envelope sent first class and bearing the logo of Yorkshire Woollens. As usual, he scooped it up and waited until he was halfway to the office before pulling off into a garage forecourt to see what it contained. The contents did not really come as a surprise. The company had experienced real difficulties in the past two years. Last year they'd closed one of the spinning mills with the loss of over 200 jobs. Peter remembered Susan reading about it in the Yorkshire Post.

'Your job's safe, isn't it?' she'd asked. It was the beginning of her suspicions that Peter might be worried about money.

'I'll be the last to go,' he'd said. 'They can't do without me.'

And he thought she'd believed him, but it had been clear to Peter that more drastic cutbacks would be required sooner or later.

Today's letter, addressed to HQ office staff, set down the financial background and the extent of the layoffs that would now be required. A staff meeting was arranged for 10.00 tomorrow morning to be followed by individual meetings with Department Heads and HR.

Peter didn't have a good feeling about how the day might work out. In his heart he knew that the department was overstaffed, and he was one of the higher paid staff – after all, he checked the salary schedules. And he knew better than anyone how his performance had slipped over the last few years, his long lunch hours, his frequent absences, his failures to concentrate. The next day he had a strong sense of foreboding as he parked in his allocated space (for how much longer?) and crossed the yard to the office.

The building was full of rumour and almost no-one was able to concentrate on work. Peter occupied himself, as he did every day, by checking stock and commodity prices. The ten o'clock meeting confirmed his worst fears for the company. Over one hundred HQ staff would have to be "let go". His meeting afterwards with the Head of Accounts and HR confirmed his worst fears.

'Peter, we'll be really sorry to see you go. We're not unappreciative of all the hard work you've put in over the years. You'll understand why we have to ask you to clear your desk this morning; you know what security's like.'

Like two undertakers they intoned the details of the settlement. Finally, they stood up to shake his hand. 'Sorry again, Peter. Good luck. Goodbye.'

'Thank you,' he said. He didn't want any confrontation. After ten years he would walk away with eighteen grand and a second-hand Volvo. Well, sod them. Financially he couldn't care less and deep down he knew he would have made the same decision if he'd been Head of Accounting. Nonetheless it hurt; the office had been a large part of his life. He'd miss the familiarity of the working days, the month end, the annual accounts.

He packed his few belongings into a cardboard box and dumped the lot in the boot of the Volvo, all the time wondering what he would say to Susan. He didn't need to go home immediately. Instead, he drove into Leeds, collected a few items from Sutcliffe Mailing, and made his way round the corner past the short-term car park to the Queens Hotel, its comfortable old fashioned interior at once familiar and nurturing. He sank into one of the large leather armchairs in the bar, to think. He ordered a coffee rather than a whisky. He knew he needed a clear head. Susan… Susan…

Susan would panic. Her entire life, their life, their home, their children's future, everything was threatened. She'd think Peter would have to find another job as soon as possible. This, surely, was the crisis Peter had been fantasising about for years, where he would unveil the details of the vast wealth which he had tended and cared for like a secret garden for just this sort of emergency. Quite how he could explain this without revealing the scale of his deceit he had no idea. The trouble was, it wasn't only the deceit, it was the implication that he hadn't trusted Susan, he had doubted her judgement, her abilities and he had preferred to keep her horizons limited to the flower shop and the semi-detached in Harrogate. He had denied her, and the children, come to that, the opportunity of living a larger and more exciting life. He didn't know how to break the news, but break it he must, this evening. Otherwise, whatever would he say in the morning when it became time for him to go to work? It had to be tonight. He rehearsed a few possibilities until it was time to head for home but couldn't get the story straight. He thought he'd wait until after dinner, when the children would be in their rooms and he would have Susan to himself.

But no such luck. No sooner was Peter through the door than Susan was putting on her coat and giving instructions about dinner and children.

'You haven't forgotten, have you? I'm baby-sitting for Emma. You know what she's like. I daren't be late. Dinner's in the oven. Daniel's got to finish his geography assignment – it has to be handed in tomorrow. Katy'll help with the clearing away, then she can watch TV, but she must be in bed before ten o'clock. I'll be late – after midnight. Don't wait up. I'll say goodnight now.'

'But… but there's something really important I need to talk to you about.'

'Well, it'll just have to wait until tomorrow, won't it?' She put her arms around him, kissed him on the cheek, and swept out of the door.

Peter came close to catching her by the arm. His one real opportunity to break his news had gone. He spent the evening in a panic, opposing thoughts colliding in his head. He didn't know what to do. He couldn't tell Susan in the morning, not with the kids around and everyone getting ready to go out. Nor could he stay at home in the morning. He'd have to go out at 8.30am as usual or they'd wonder what he was doing. But then it dawned on him. So long as he left home and returned at his usual times, would Susan suspect anything? Did he really have to tell Susan anything at this stage? Did he have to tell her anything ever? His thoughts started to coalesce into a pattern. He still felt nervous but had a whisky and went to bed soon after the children. When Susan arrived home, he pretended to be asleep.

In the morning the alarm went as usual. Everything had to be normal. Susan went to have a shower. Once breakfast was over, the children got ready for school, and Susan got ready to go to the flower shop.

Peter followed his usual routine. He got up, had breakfast, got in the car and drove off at 8.30.

At first, he simply took his usual route to work, but after two miles the road divided and he took the right fork to Leeds. There he would build a new professional existence. He would take on the persona of the character he felt he was becoming – a successful investor, a wealthy businessman, a man of means. He parked near the station and walked round to Sutcliffe Mailing. He needed their help until he could make new arrangements.

Three months later, Peter was sitting in his new office, a penthouse overlooking Leeds city centre. He felt pleased with himself. Sutcliffe mailing had agreed to let him use their spare office until he was able to set himself up properly. Every day he had driven into Leeds, then back to Harrogate in the evening. Away from his old comfy existence in the accounts office, and buoyed by his new freedom, he had a growing confidence in his abilities. Using his business vehicle, ABZ Investments, he had leased a serviced office in a prestigious new development. This morning he had parked in his own numbered space in the basement, collected a latte and pain-au-raison from the coffee bar (he loved these little luxuries), and said hello to the pretty assistant, Chloe, who would be coming to see him later to discuss the administrative arrangements.

He didn't think Susan suspected anything. There had been a bad moment early on when news of the redundancies at Yorkshire Woollens had hit the local paper, but he had been ready for it.

'You never mentioned there've been more redundancies at Yorkshire Woollens.' Susan pushed the Yorkshire

Evening News across the worktop as Peter came into the kitchen.

'Didn't I? Well, the press so often crank things up to be worse than they are.' Peter picked up the paper and skipped through the article. 'They say over a hundred staff at Headquarters. It's nonsense. I suppose if you include vacancies and temps, and also the cleaners and catering staff that have been outsourced, you could get it up to a hundred, but that's pushing it.'

'So, your job's still all right then?'

'Oh, God, yes. Don't you worry. I'll probably do well out of it. More responsibilities. We'll be fine. What's for dinner?'

The lies were becoming more fluent, bolder. He'd got away with it again.

Everything had been in place for a few months now and he could spend more of his time researching investment opportunities and finding increasingly clever ways to reduce his tax liabilities. There was also the opportunity to start living a bit more like a man of means, like having a decent lunch for instance. He thought he would try Sous Le Ney, a discreet and cosy French bistro just round the corner. A pity to go on his own. Perhaps he could persuade Chloe to join him one day, but it was good to try the place out on his own first. He wouldn't have much appetite left by the evening…

Susan's mobile switched straight to voicemail, so it was easy for him. 'Oh, hello darling. Just ringing to say not to bother with dinner for me tonight. I'm having lunch in the canteen. Hope all's well. See you later. Love you.'

He'd never used the canteen when he was there.

Susan… Susan… it was Susan who was the problem. The weight of falsehood was growing almost daily. Fortunately, he had never told her much about his work in the past, never really involved her, and to be fair she had never seemed to take any interest. Nonetheless, work had hardly been a secret, and now it was. The more time went on the more of a fictitious construct his days were becoming. He could feel the weight of it depressing his home life. It was not so bad with the kids. He was happy spending time with them in the evenings, helping with homework, buying them gifts and treats. So long as they were around, he could have a good time with Susan too – they could join in the same things, eat together – he was always keen to eat with the children. It was the evenings alone with Susan which he found increasingly uncomfortable, the silences, frightened of saying the wrong thing, of what Susan might come up with, any conversation which included household finances, or anything to do with work, or any mention of Leeds. The veil of lies hanging over his daily life showed signs of wear and tear. A couple of times Susan had read text messages on his mobile, initially mistaking it for hers:

In Zurich today: will confirm sale on return, Rupert.

'Text from someone called Rupert,' she'd said, handing the phone to him, question marks in her eyebrows, and another time:

Please confirm 12.00 your office OK for tomorrow. Felicity.

'Ooh! Felicity!'

And then there'd been the parking tickets and receipts – all from Leeds – in the pockets of his raincoat when Susan had taken it to the cleaners. She'd left them in a heap on the bedside table. Had she looked at them? Still beating himself up inside, still distracted, he took the lift down to the lobby. Chloe got in at the eighth floor wearing a pencil thin dark green dress, smart strappy heels, and a shoulder bag from Mulberry.

'Hello, Mr. Goldsmith, how are you settling in?'

'Very well, Chloe, thank you, and please call me Peter.'

He could smell her perfume. His eyes traced her profile in the mirrored walls as the floors clicked downwards to the ground. The doors opened and he waved her forwards. Peter followed her through the lobby and out onto the pavement.

'See you later then,' he said.

Chloe tossed her lovely head. 'Yes, see you later, Mr Goldsmith. Sorry, I mean Peter.'

He smiled, felt a tremor of pleasure, and turned round to head up the street, straight into Sasha. This time there was no looking away, no pretending not to have noticed.

'Peter, fancy seeing you here.' Sasha had one eye on Peter and the other watching Chloe's retreating figure.

'Sasha, what a surprise. What brings you to Leeds. Shopping I expect?'

'No, I have a new job just round the corner at the tax office. Didn't Susan tell you? Actually, I told Susan I thought I saw you before, but she said I must have been mistaken.'

There was no way out, but he tried. 'I don't come into Leeds very often. Actually, this is a bit of a secret shopping trip of my own. It's coming up to our wedding anniversary; I'm looking for something special. Don't tell Susan you saw me, will you?'

'It's not really any of my business,' she said. 'When's your anniversary then? Are you doing anything special?'

'I expect we'll go out somewhere,' he said, looking at his watch. 'Sorry, I've got to go; my parking ticket's about to expire.'

He set off towards the multi-storey car park. Sous Le Ney would have to wait. Had Sasha believed him? There was nothing he could do if she didn't. He would have to brazen it out. Meanwhile, he'd have to take greater care at lunchtimes. Sasha was a bloody nuisance.

Weeks passed. No mention was made of Sasha, but something was up, he could tell. Susan became more remote; conversation was restricted to the most mundane subjects. He often felt Susan looking at him as if curious to know what he might do or say next. He dared not ask her what was the matter.

He did not have to wait very long to find out. It was a Tuesday morning. Susan's day off work. Peter was going for an early lunch. Emerging from the lift into the lobby he saw Susan approaching the revolving door in the entrance. He quickly retreated through a side door into the passage leading to the restrooms. Peeping through the small window panel, he saw Susan cross the lobby and approach the reception desk. She wore a dark grey suit over a silk blouse, the highest of heels and carried an attaché case. He strained his ears. She was asking for him.

'I'm his wife.'

The receptionist looked up from her screen. 'Oh.' The surprise was quickly suppressed. 'I'll see if he's in.' Then 'I'm sorry, he must be at lunch. Was he expecting you?'

Susan didn't respond, and after the tiniest hesitation the receptionist added, 'I don't know how long he'll be.'

'It doesn't matter,' said Susan. 'I'll wait.'

She walked over to the stylish arrangement of chairs and potted plants, picked up a copy of the Yorkshire Post and sat down. She was no more than two yards from where Peter was leaning against the side door.

It was no good. He couldn't stay hiding in the corridor outside the toilets all afternoon. The game was up anyway. He pushed open the door and walked slowly and quietly to stand in front of Susan.

'Susan,' he said softly.

She raised her eyes, carefully folded the newspaper onto the seat beside her, and stood up straight facing him. She was very calm. 'Shall we go to your office?'

He pressed the button for the lift, then the button for the twenty-first floor. There was just the two of them. The lift hissed quietly upwards. Inside, silence. Susan looked at Peter in the mirror; Peter looked at the floor.

He unlocked the office and stood aside. Susan walked across to the window, looking out over the city and the surrounding hills. She ran her fingers across the polished mahogany of the desk, brushed the leaves of the orange blossom tree in its enormous terracotta urn, stroked the leather of the sofa.

'Well, do you have anything to say?'

Peter's mind had been racing since first seeing Susan down in the lobby. How much did she know? He scrambled together an explanation.

'You know when Yorkshire Woollens made all those people redundant last year?' He looked straight into her eyes. He surprised himself by the boldness of the story he was about to tell and the calmness of his delivery. He had regained control. 'Well, I was one of them. I couldn't tell you Susan. I wanted to but when it came to it, I couldn't.'

He paused for effect. 'But I didn't know what to do. For days I pretended to go off to work as normal, but I couldn't keep it up. The more time went on the worse I felt.' He looked at her to see how she was reacting, but she was blank, waiting. The big lie was still to come.

'But the redundancy package was really good, 'cause of my long service and then I thought I could set myself up with a small business of my own using the redundancy money and,' he gestured around the room, 'here it is. Not so grand as it looks, but I think I'll be able to make a go of it. I'm so sorry I never told you. I should have told you right away, obviously, but then it was too late. I was always going to tell you. I've been such a fool,' he finished rather lamely.

Towards the end of his explanation Peter had come to realise that Susan was unnaturally quiet. She hadn't interrupted once. There was a faint expression of disgust on her face.

'And that's it, is it?' she asked.

'We'll be all right, Susan.' He managed to look eager, started to get back into gear. 'I think I'll be able to earn enough for us to get by. We won't have to sell the house or anything.'

Susan still had this look of disgust. Something somewhere was ticking waiting to go off.

'So how much do you have?'

'From the redundancy? Nearly fifty grand.'

'And how much do we have in our saving account.'

'About another twelve.'

'I thought so. So, you've put the redundancy money into another account?'

'Well, yes. It's in an account for the new business.'

'In your name?'

'Er, yes.'

He stopped and looked again at her face. She had been on the edge of tears and he stepped forward in alarm but then there was a sudden frown. She dashed the back of her hand across her eyes.

'Get away from me.' The words were spat out in a great fury.

She faced him and shouted, 'Why can't you tell the truth for once? You must think I'm an idiot. All these years you've lied and lied.'

He shook his head, convincingly, he thought. 'I don't know what you mean.'

'Oh, don't you?' She shouted at him again, 'Do I have to spell it out for you.'

Susan trembled a little. When she next spoke, her voice was low and shaky but had the momentum of a goods train behind it. 'What about all the money you inherited from your gran? That was the start of it, wasn't it? All these years you've lived a lie.'

'You knew about the inheritance?' His mouth dropped open.

'Only recently. My God if I'd only known about it at the time. And you've kept it secret for six years. Every day you've lived a lie, and even now you're still trying to hide it.'

Peter didn't know where to look. In the end he looked out of the window. Susan clearly knew more, far more than he'd realised. He didn't know how to recover. He needed to think but he was jerked back by Susan.

'Look at me, damn you. All this time…' she repeated.

'I was saving it until we really needed it,' he said.

'And you couldn't trust me with the knowledge?'

'It's not that.'

'Oh, no? I mean, it's not as if you simply forgot to tell me is it, or thought "I'll tell her tomorrow, or next week, or next Christmas"? No, you went to a huge amount of trouble to hide it away, didn't you? Like some miserable bloody miser. Private mailboxes, foreign bank accounts, your own special laptop.'

'I was just being prudent, Susan.'

'Prudent?' She shouted so loudly that he jumped back. His ears rang. 'And what about when I wanted Mum to move nearer to us, when she was ill? Remember?'

He stood silent.

'Remember?' She shouted at the top of her voice. It seemed as if the whole building was stood still, listening. 'But you said we didn't have the money. That was being prudent, was it? Prudent with your money. You think it's all yours? For richer for poorer, Peter, for richer for poorer.'

'But that's what would have happened if I'd told you,' Peter said. 'We'd have spent the money and now we'd be no better off. Susan, you've got to understand, we're worth a fortune.'

'To spend on what? The children's schooling – oh, but that's too late. The flower shop? You bastard, you told me we couldn't afford a loan. You've lied and lied. It's not the way a marriage works, Peter.'

'What do you mean?'

'I mean it's over. Our marriage. Over.' She shouted at him again, in sudden bursts of anger, like driving in a post with a mallet; his head jerked with every blow. 'This afternoon you will go home and pack your things. We'll explain to the children together; I can't trust you to say anything on your own. Sleep on a park bench or check yourself into a fancy hotel, I don't care. We will get a divorce. I want half of everything you have plus maintenance.'

'For God's sake, Susan. You can't go through with this. Everything I've done has been for you and the children.'

'Don't give me that,' she cut him off. 'I can never believe you again. I can't live with someone as deceitful as you, and don't think for a moment that you can hide things from me any longer. I know about the inheritance, I know about your old hidey hole at Sutcliffe Mailing – I've been to see them, dammit. Your redundancy? I've phoned your boss. You can bet how shocked he was. And three months ago, I found the password on your laptop, lucky1983, the year of our marriage you two-faced bastard. And Sasha's done a grand job for me on all your wheeling and dealings, the tax dodges, ABZ Investments, the offshore holdings.'

Peter slumped down in the chair behind the desk, his head in his hands. He looked up, a flash of anger, a fox caught in its lair.

‘Sasha’s behind this isn’t she?’

‘Of course not, you fool. But it was when you denied Sasha saw you in Leeds that I knew you were lying. I’d been suspicious for a long time. I’d found parking tickets in your pockets, weird messages on your phone, strange emails. Once I thought you had another woman.’ She laughed, her hand on her forehead. ‘I’m not sure if that might have been better, at least easier to understand. That was when I started to trace it all backwards. Everything fell into place.

Peter sat with his eyes closed, then he shook his head as if to rid himself of a bad dream.

‘OK,’ he said. ‘Have it your way. I won’t argue with you now. You’re overwrought. I’ll go home and pack a bag, but let’s not do anything rash. We can talk about the future when you’re in a calmer frame of mind.’

Susan recognised the signs, the unwillingness to engage, the apparent backing down, the condescension. He was already plotting, scheming how to rescue the marriage as well as his fortune.

‘No way, Peter. There’s no way back from this and let me warn you now: do not think you can hide anything any longer, not a single penny. Your precious laptop is locked away in Sasha’s office. She has details of all your accounts, everywhere. And we have a fat file documenting all your tax affairs. One false move from you and, so help me God, I’ll pass it to the Inland Revenue.’

It was the first time she had seen him look genuinely frightened.

‘It’s over,’ she said. ‘Can’t you see, you bloody fool, it’s over.’

NATIVITY

The nativity play was especially successful this year. All of us proud parents had applauded. We'd sung along; never before had the church hall resounded quite so beautifully with carols. When we sang *Hark the Herald Angels Sing* at the end it was as if the whole company of angels was singing with us.

The angels were a bit of a surprise for everyone. The stage was dark because it was supposed to be night, and early on in the performance, when Mary and Joseph had walked on from stage right, Katie had appeared, stage left, as the angel Gabriel. She was perched on a platform made from one of the tables covered in a big black cloth. She had white wings, decorated with real feathers, with sequins and all, really beautiful, which Mrs Melksham had made, and she had a long white glistening robe from the dressing up box and her golden halo. Shortly afterwards she was joined by two other angels, much higher up above the stage at the back of the auditorium. They must have been suspended by wires. It was all very effective, very convincing. I think Katie was a bit surprised. She kept looking up, but they smiled and gestured to her to get on with her act, which she performed very well, come to think of it, saying Mary would have a son and call his name Emmanuel, and all that.

She might have forgotten Emmanuel, but she looked up as if for support, and one of the angels mouthed the word for her and she remembered just in time. And when she'd finished and backed off into the darkness, flapping her wings slowly and carefully and disappearing behind the side curtain, the other angels seemed to fly away upwards. How they did it I'll never know.

But that was nothing to what they did later, after the shepherds and the wise men – Darren was one of the wise men, he looked so handsome in his red velvet robe – had done their thing. When they reached the finale and all the players were on the stage grouped around the manger, dozens – and I mean dozens – of angels descended from the roof. How they got up there in the first place heaven only knows. And like the earlier angels they must have been on wires because they sort of hovered in the air above the manger. They were all jostling around because there was barely room for them all. I don't know who they were. They must have been from one of the other Sunday School groups, tho' the vicar seemed as surprised as the rest of us. Well, could they sing, or what? They were fantastic. Their voices were the sweetest you've heard, and like I said, when they joined everyone else in singing *Hark the Herald Angels Sing*, it was like heaven had come to earth. Several Mums I saw were in tears with the sheer beauty.

Afterwards everyone was talking about it. One of the dads works for a music company and he was going around all important saying he had to find out who these people were so he could sign them up, but I don't think he's found out to this day.

Oh, and I just remembered another really strange thing, quite eerie somehow. At the end, when everyone was still on stage and the angels were still hovering about, there was the crying of a baby. You'd never guess, but there was a real baby in the crib. It's caused a terrible stir because no-one knows whose it is. Mary – or rather Amy, who played Mary – had a doll dressed up as baby Jesus, and she'd put it in the manger, but someone somehow had substituted it with the real thing. It must have been done whilst the angels were singing, because everyone was looking up at them and crying. Amy said she wanted to call the child Emmanuel, as instructed by the angel. She said he would be the light of the world. Would you believe it?

ABOUT THE AUTHOR

William Wilson pursued a business career and travelled extensively before retiring in 2003. He subsequently took a BA Fine Art degree course, graduating from Brighton University in 2010, followed by Creative Writing Course with New Writing South. He is a widower with two daughters and four grandchildren, and lives in Hove.

LIKE TO READ MORE WORK LIKE THIS?

Then sign up to our mailing list and download our free collection of short stories, *Magnetism*. Sign up now to receive this free e-book and also to find out about all of our new publications and offers.

Sign up here:
http://eepurl.com/gbpdVz

PLEASE LEAVE A REVIEW

Reviews are so important to writers. Please take the time to review this book. A couple of lines is fine.

Reviews help the book to become more visible to buyers. Retailers will promote books with multiple reviews.

This in turn helps us to sell more books… And then we can afford to publish more books like this one.

Leaving a review is very easy.

Go to https://smarturl.it/zukzak, scroll down the left-hand side of the Amazon page and click on the "Write a customer review" button.

OTHER PUBLICATIONS BY BRIDGE HOUSE

Speculations

by Stephen Faulkner

What if?

All good stories and novels begin very simply when the author asks the question, "What if…?" In the fourteen stories in Speculations the author offers each solution while leaving it up to you to figure out the "what if…?" question that each tale alludes to.

Each story is an intriguing journey into the realms of imagination, fantasy and the incredible. Some of the places you will be taken in this book include the inner mind of a creature that remains on Earth long after the human race has been eliminated; a world that exports a tasty treat that originates in a quite unsavoury place; and an all-knowing, all powerful alien machine which can do literally anything at all.

Order from Amazon:

ISBN: 978-1-914199-08-0 (paperback)
978-1-914199-09-7 (ebook)

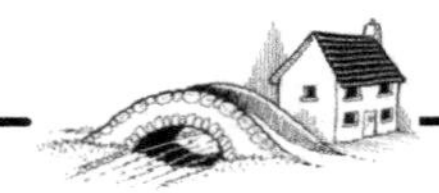

Mysterious Ways

by Jeff Laurents

Mimsie Fotheringey's attitude to men? "Use them then lose them" was her motto. A modern day Adam and Eve undergo a repellant physical change. Is Emily Mayhew's real motivation about buying a house, or are her wants and needs a little more complex to say the least? Homes Under the Hammer takes on a new twist as people attend a unique auction to delight in the gruesome fate of the former residents of the properties on offer.

Mysterious Ways is a single author collection from Bridge House Publishing. Jeff Laurents is an enthralling story-teller who invites us to look again at what we thought was normal.

Order from Amazon:

ISBN: 978-1-914199-04-2 (paperback)
978-1-914199-05-9 (ebook)

Wishful Thinking

by Derek Corbett

A collection of stories in which justice is not always done but leaves room for some wishful thinking.

Relationships break down and are sometimes saved by money. Snowdrops bring precious memories. Brothers in a religious order have to find a way through some difficult decisions.

Wishful Thinking is a single-author collection from Bridge House Publishing. Derek Corbett takes the reader gently by the hand and offers us the comfort of a good story well told.

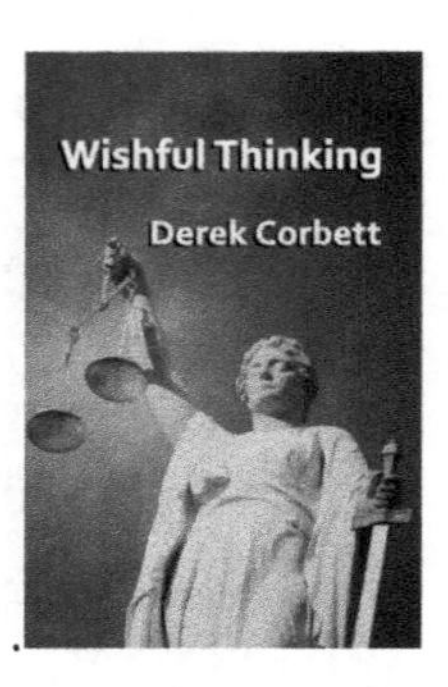

"An amazing collection of short stories, with a novella called *Glady's Time* thrown in too." (*Amazon*)

Order from Amazon:

ISBN: 978-1-907335-98-3 (paperback)
978-1-907335-99-0 (ebook)

Lightning Source UK Ltd.
Milton Keynes UK
UKHW021051161122
412293UK00008B/85